Silence of the Dead
A Jackson & Dallas Thriller
By L.J. Sellers

SILENCE OF THE DEAD

Cover art by David MacFarlane

ISBN: 978-1-7345418-3-0
Published in the USA by Spellbinder Press

Cast of Characters:

Wade Jackson: detective/Violent Crimes Unit

Katie Jackson: Jackson's daughter

Kera Kollmorgan: Jackson's girlfriend/nurse

Lara Evans: detective/task force member

Rob Schakowski (Schak): detective/task force member

Michael Quince: detective/task force member

Denise Lammers: Jackson's supervisor/sergeant

Sergeant Bruckner: SWAT unit leader

Jamie Dallas: FBI undercover specialist

Rich Gunderson: medical examiner/attends crime scenes

Rudolph Konrad: pathologist/performs autopsies

Zena Summers: murder victim

Dagen Hammersmith: Zena's boyfriend/suspect

Lisha Hammersmith: Dagen's mother/suspect

Ruby Bannon: victim's landlady

Darren Mitchell: slain police officer

Jove Goddard: cult leader

Augie Goddard: Jove's son

Chapter 1

Thursday, Oct. 1, 9:36 a.m.

Detective Wade Jackson hurried into the conference room and took a seat, his body tense. Meetings that involved all the detectives in the Violent Crimes Unit were never good—usually new rules to follow—but this one had been called only a few minutes ago. *Shit was going down somewhere.*

"Listen up!" Sergeant Lammers bellowed from the front, her six-foot body expanding the volume. "I have bad news. Officer Darren Mitchell was shot in the head this morning as he made an arrest."

Jackson inhaled sharply. He'd never met the patrol cop, but a wave of sadness washed over him.

Lammers waited for the murmurs and cursing to subside, then held up a hand. "I'm sorry to report that Mitchell died on the way to the hospital, but the suspect is in custody."

"How the hell did it happen?" Jackson asked. Their training was supposed to prevent those tragic deaths.

"We don't know yet." Lammers' voice was tight. "The arrestee, Dominic Bulgar, has a history of drug crimes and violent assault, but there's some confusion about where the shot came from."

A chill ran up Jackson's spine. None of them were safe. Half the population seemed to have lost their minds and morality.

"I'm taking the lead on the investigation," the sergeant continued. 'I'll handle as much as I can, but I need help from all of you. Please prioritize whatever tasks I assign."

She hadn't needed to say it. Apprehending a cop killer always came first. Jackson was glad he didn't have an active murder investigation going. He and his team had wrapped up a case a few days earlier, and he'd finally finished writing the reports late yesterday. He would be able to take on whatever the sergeant threw at him.

"The shooter is most likely the perp we already have in custody, but it's also possible that it was someone connected to him who was at the house when the officer arrived."

"Or anyone with a grudge against Mitchell," someone mumbled.

"Right. So I need everyone to look back through old cases for other potential suspects, then send the leads to me." Lammers locked eyes on Jackson. "I need you to find his wife and break the news, then ask her who might have a personal grudge."

The worst possible assignment. "What's her name?"

"Sloan Mitchell. I'll give you access to Darren Mitchell's personnel file so you can peruse it for anything that pops."

Jackson nodded.

Lammers looked to the end of the back row at Rob Schakowski. "Schak, I want you to join me for the suspect's interrogation. Meet me downstairs in twenty minutes."

"Will do." Schak nodded his buzz-cut head.

Jackson would have preferred to conduct the interrogation, but they were all a team and it didn't matter. Lammers continued to hand out assignments, then announced, "We'll meet back here at seven this evening. Get some dinner beforehand." She gestured for the group to leave. "Be safe!"

As other detectives stood, Jackson sat for a moment, processing the news of the officer's death. The department had lost three men to the pandemic that year, and others had quit or retired, including two detectives. Which explained why Lammers was heading the investigation. She knew other cases would keep coming, and they would all be working round the clock until the cop killer was apprehended.

"Are you okay?"

Jackson glanced up and saw Lara Evans, her heart-shaped face solemn, her athletic body tense. Just the sight of her made him feel better about the human species, which he'd lost a lot of faith in recently.

"Yep." Jackson stood, and they walked out together. Knowing he would be working those late nights with Evans eased some of his stress. She'd started in the Violent Crimes Unit five years earlier, and his attraction had been immediate. But as her mentor, he'd shelved those feeling, then he'd met Kera shortly after. They'd fallen in love and dated happily for years. But life had thrown them one curveball after another, each taking a toll. Their forced separation had been the worst, and during that time, Jackson's feelings for Evans had resurfaced.

He'd recently spoken with a counselor for the first time in his life and confessed how much he loved Evans, which had only intensified his internal conflict. He and Kera were about to move into a rental together. If he didn't make the break now, he would settle into a life with her and their boys—and never know if an intimate relationship with Evans could work.

They reached their cubicles on the second floor, and Evans patted his shoulder. "Sorry you got the grim duty."

"Lammers must be mad at me."

"She knows you're good at it."

Footsteps sounded, and Evans pivoted to Schak as he approached. "She gave you the interrogation because she thinks you're too old and fat to be out in the field." Evans winked at their barrel-shaped teammate.

"I am." Schak grunted. "My feet can't take that door-to-door shit anymore."

"I'd better get on it." Evans sounded energetic as usual. "Officers are at the scene now, waiting for me to coordinate the neighborhood interviews." She gave a small wave and walked toward the stairs leading down to the back parking lot.

"I have to find the widow." Jackson sighed and stepped into his cubicle.

At his desk, he opened the link Lammers had sent, accessed Darren Mitchell's personnel file, and quickly found his spouse: *Sloan Mitchell, age 35, self-employed life coach.* Jackson jotted down her details, including home address, on the old-school pocket notebook he still carried. He called her phone number, but a voice message picked up: "This is Sloan, and I'd like to help you find your path. I'm sorry I missed your call. Leave me a message, and I'll get right back to you."

Jackson hesitated. He needed to speak with her in person, but he couldn't do that until he tracked her down. "It's Detective Jackson, and I'm headed to your home now. Please wait for me there." *Ominous and vague.* She would know it was bad news. He stood and braced himself for the task ahead.

The upscale home in the South University neighborhood was bigger and fancier than Jackson had expected. On a cop's salary, Mitchell probably hadn't been able to afford it alone, so his wife was likely doing well with her business. *Life coach. Hah!* What a racket. But Jackson hoped whatever skills she'd developed would help her cope with her husband's death.

No vehicles were in the driveway, but the three-car garage might be full. Jackson hurried to the door and rang the bell, but instinct told him no one was home. Too quiet. He waited, pressed the buzzer again, then pounded on the door. "Detective Jackson, Eugene Police."

After a few more minutes, he left Sloan another voice message, then headed back to his sedan. *What now?* He couldn't just wait for her to return. She might be out of town, or anywhere.

A young boy walked up the street. Jackson hoped it wasn't the Mitchells' son, but he hadn't noticed any kids in the personnel file. Stress and guilt roiled in his gut. He and Kera had two young boys in their care—children who had already experienced abandonment—and they would be traumatized if he broke up their family. *They were still preschoolers,* Jackson reminded himself. The boys would handle it better now than later.

He started the engine and headed for his house a few miles away. Kera had the day off and was likely home alone. He had to tell her *now.* They were scheduled to sign the rental agreement tomorrow.

Jackson's heart pounded as he stepped into the house he'd lived in most of his life. At least now, he wouldn't have to move. Kera stood in the kitchen, an empty cardboard box on the floor beside her. *She was packing already.* Tears welled in his eyes.

"Wade. What's going on?" She moved toward him, concern in her eyes.

Damn, she was striking. Tall, with long bronze hair, wide cheekbones, and full lips. And so loving. Could he really do this to her? She had already lost so much—her son in the war, then both parents recently to cancer. In his therapy session, Jackson had come to realize that he'd stayed in the relationship too long out of guilt and fear that his rejection might be Kera's breaking point.

Jackson blinked back the tears. "Uh, a patrol officer was shot and killed this morning."

Kera hugged him. "I'm so sorry to hear that."

He squeezed her hard, knowing it might be the last time, then stepped back. He had to tell her. But the look in her eyes stopped him. Something was going on, and the house was too quiet. Benjie was in preschool, but her grandson should have been there. "Where's Micah?"

"Still at Daniel's.

That was odd. Kera's ex-husband had been out of the picture for years, then a few months earlier, he'd suddenly started asking to spend time with the boy.

"He kept Micah and served me with papers this morning," Kera said. "He's filing for full custody."

Jackson's jaw dropped open. "No shit? Just like that?"

"He says Micah is happier with him and doesn't want to come back here."

"Do you believe it?"

"I don't know. Daniel probably gives him everything he wants and lets him eat junk food." Kera's lips trembled.

"Micah's been upset and acting out ever since I took him to California to care for my parents. But what else could I do?"

"This isn't your fault." Jackson tried to be comforting. "Daniel is just being a selfish dick. Does he really think he has a chance in court?"

"Apparently so. He's hired a top-notch custody lawyer."

"I'm so sorry. We can fight this. It'll be expensive, but I know how much you love that boy."

Kera blinked back tears. "Maybe Daniel will settle for joint custody."

That could be a good thing, less pressure on him. Jackson hated himself for the thought. How could he break up with Kera now? Yet he didn't have the time, money, or energy for a custody battle—especially for a child who wasn't his and didn't want to bond with him. Overwhelmed, Jackson felt blood pound in his ears.

"I'm sorry I bothered you with this in the middle of your workday." Kera straightened her shoulders. "It's my issue, and I'll deal with it."

Jackson's phone rang in his jacket pocket, and relief washed over him. He snatched it up and looked at the screen: *Sergeant Lammers.* "I have to take this." He turned away from Kera, barely able to breathe, and picked up the call. "What have you got?"

"Another homicide."

A sharp pain in his chest. "An officer?"

"No. A young woman found dead at the top of Skinner's Butte. Blood on her neck and arms."

Almost as bad. "Any ID?"

"Not yet."

"Who called it in?"

"A man out for his morning walk. His dog found the body about thirty feet down from the parking lot."

"Is the caller still at the scene?"

"Probably not. He said he had to go to work, but I'll text you his name, phone number, and place of employment."

"Thanks." The guy wasn't a likely suspect, but they would question him at some point anyway. "I know we're stretched thin. Do I get a team?"

"Yes, but you'll all be working both cases." Her voice tightened. "Did you notify Officer Mitchell's wife?"

"Not yet. I stopped by, but she wasn't home, so I left her a vague message."

"I'll see if I can track her down. Go work the new crime scene, and we'll catch up at the taskforce meeting tonight."

"On my way."

Chapter 2

Jackson passed the turnoff and had to circle the block. Access to the butte was tucked away in a quaint neighborhood between the county jail and a riverside park and was easy to miss. After making the turn the second time, he forced himself to drive slowly on the narrow road as it circled up the steep hill. On the backside, he spotted a teenage boy on a path leading down to the rock climbing area and a jogger coming down a path from the top. One more curve, and the lane flattened into a parking area overlooking Eugene's downtown blocks and south hills. A favorite place for couples to gaze at the night lights while they partied. The whole butte was an attraction to young people.

A dark-blue patrol SUV blocked the access at both ends of the lot, a limited response. Everyone else on duty was likely searching for Officer Mitchell's killer or associates. Jackson stopped behind Evans' city-issued sedan and climbed out. She obviously hadn't missed the turnoff. As her mentor and teammate, he admired her sharpness and physical agility. But as a potential lover who was ten years younger, would she make him feel inadequate? If she even still had feelings for him. They'd had a candid, romantic moment one night after a traumatic case and expressed their attraction. But life had quickly interfered.

Jackson shut down his personal thoughts and focused on the scene. At first he didn't see anyone, but as he neared the main lookout area near the flagpole, he heard voices. A moment later, he spotted Evans and two patrol officers about thirty feet below on the slope. Jackson hurried down the steps that cut through a patch of scraggly late-summer dried grass.

Evans pivoted toward him. "It's about time." She gave a small smile, then held out a denim pouch with a long strap. "I found her ID in this." Evans pointed to a large rock nearby. "Over there."

"Who is she?" Jackson pulled latex gloves from his shoulder bag.

"Zena Summers, age eighteen. No phone. Just her ID, lip gloss, and a key."

Jackson reached for the bag, then stared at the photo on the state-issued ID card. She had ash-brown hair, hazel eyes, and dimples—plus a pretty smile. Thankfully, he wouldn't have to look too closely at the dead girl's face. That was always excruciating. He turned to the patrol officers. "Anything to add?"

The tall man stepped forward. "Officer Markham."

Jackson had met him, but couldn't remember when or where.

"Two teenage boys were in the parking lot when I arrived. They took off running down the path." Markham pointed at a narrow trail that circled around the butte. "I yelled for them to stop, but they were out of sight almost immediately, and I didn't want to leave the crime scene."

A flash of worry in Jackson's gut. "What did they look like?"

Markham tensed. "Both were skinny and dark haired. One had on shorts and a white T-shirt with some kind of decal, and the other wore jeans and a gray hoodie."

The teenager he'd spotted on the way up. Irritated that witnesses—or suspects—had been allowed to flee, Jackson snapped, "I saw the guy in the gray hoodie over by the rock climbing area. Go pick him up!"

Jackson glanced at the female officer. "Put out an ATL for both, then start searching this area. If the victim had a phone, we need to find it." Jackson wasn't optimistic. The attempt-to-locate on the kids would take a backseat to Mitchell's case, and cell phones almost never turned up at death scenes.

As the patrol cops jogged up the hill, Jackson finally spotted the victim. Her body lay horizontal in the middle of a circular, low-to-the ground framework. He stepped over the narrow plank and realized the shape was oval. A twelve-foot O, painted yellow for the University of Oregon. Eugene's mini-version of the famous Hollywood sign. Had she been dumped here? Was the location significant to the perp? If her death was even a crime.

As Evans stepped into the oval, an engine rumbled on the road above them. Probably evidence techs, or maybe the medical examiner. Jackson had to get a look at the body right now. He and Evans squatted on either side of the girl, taking photos as they looked her over. Jackson guessed her to be about five-seven with an average build. She wore black yoga pants, a white crop-top, and pink slip-on shoes. His daughter had been dressed almost identically this morning. Would he ever be able to look at a young female victim without feeling how devastated he would be if it were Katie?

Jackson picked up one of the girl's pale hands. No rigor mortis yet, and no defensive wounds. But she had a bruise on her wrist, where someone might have grabbed her too tightly. He checked her other hand, startled to discover she was missing a chunk of her pinkie finger. "Look at this." He held up the hand for Evans.

"Weird." Evans scowled. "I've never seen that on a woman before. Most of the time, it's a guy who got careless with tools or machinery. Or played with fireworks as a kid."

"The wound is completely scarred over, so it happened several years ago. Could have been a medical issue like a bad infection." Jackson set her hand down. "But teenage girls do stupid things too."

Evans let out a soft grunt. "I sure did. Mostly when I was partying. I almost lost a toe being drunk and stupid in the woods." She glanced back at the dead girl's face. "Check out this gash on her neck." Evans removed debris from the dried blood and slipped it into an evidence bag.

Jackson scooted left, then leaned in for a closer look. The wound ran from her ear to the hollow of her neck. It was ragged and shallow, but not life threatening. "Not a knife." He took a quick photo. The techs would take a zillion, but sometimes studying or comparing those on his phone helped his thought processes.

"It's dirty, as if caused by a tree branch," Evans said. "Or maybe the edge of a rock."

Had a crazy stranger assaulted her? Or had she been intoxicated and fallen? Jackson glanced around. The immediate area contained mostly dead grass and big rocks, but trees and shrubs covered the landscape everywhere else on the hill. Jackson forced himself to examine the girl's head, noticing a lump with a small patch of dried blood above her ear on the same side as the neck wound. "I think she either fell or was pushed."

Evans leaned in too, her face inches from his. "Neither wound seems lethal."

Jackson nodded. "She's not stiff yet, so she probably died sometime last evening."

"Hey, that's my job!"

Jackson glanced up the slope and saw Rich Gunderson, the medical examiner, coming down the steps, followed by two technicians he didn't recognize. The senior techs were likely still at Mitchell's crime scene. "As usual," Jackson said, "we need the time of death ASAP."

"Then step aside and let me get her temperature." Gunderson gestured impatiently. "Two death scenes in one day. And both probably homicides. The world has gone frigging crazy!"

Jackson and Evans stood and backed away from the body. "Let's search for whatever caused those wounds." Jackson turned to the closest boulder. "Maybe her blood is on something nearby."

"Let the techs do it," Gunderson snapped. "Neither of you is wearing booties or a hairnet. You're contaminating the scene."

Jackson started to apologize, then stopped himself. Thousands of people had tromped through this area over the years. Nothing his team did here would matter—unless they found a perpetrator and he'd left something at the scene they could match to him. Or her. Jackson stepped out of the O-shaped area and started up the steps, scanning the ground on either side. Evans walked parallel to him, about ten feet away on the grass, also searching. Near the top, Jackson picked up a cigarette butt and an empty condom package and bagged both.

"Want me to check out the address on her ID card?" Evans asked.

"Let's both go. It's only five minutes from here."

They headed for their cars. "If she lives with her family, we can get a lot accomplished," Evans commented.

His thinking too. "We need to track Zena's final movements and determine if she came up here with someone else."

"You mean a boyfriend."

"Or girlfriend."

Evans smiled. "How culturally sensitive of you."

"You can't raise a teenager now without getting in the mode."

Jackson stopped at Evans' car and watched her climb in. "See you in a bit."

Chapter 3

Jackson stood on the sidewalk, staring at the small house on Olive Street. It was old, funky, and overgrown with shrubs, ferns, and perennials, but the owner had recently added a room over the garage that was freshly painted. Evans pulled up, and they approached the bungalow together.

The door opened, and a stout woman with blonde-gray hair stepped outside. "What do you want?"

"Detectives Jackson and Evans, Eugene Police. Do you know Zena Summers?"

"She's my tenant. Why?"

Damn. This wasn't the victim's family home, and his list of people to give horrific news to was growing. "We've got some bad news. Can we come in?"

"Oh no." The woman's hand flew to her mouth. She stood for a moment with her eyes closed, then stepped back and gestured for them to step inside. "Zena didn't come home last night, and I've been worried. Is she dead?"

"Yes, unfortunately. I'm sorry."

"That's so sad." The woman's eyes watered, and she wiped away a tear. "Zena was so excited about being on her own and experiencing life."

Jackson glanced around the cluttered room, which was as overgrown with plants as her front yard. "What's your name?"

"Ruby Bannon."

As Jackson made a note, Evans asked, "Can we see Zena's room?"

"Of course." The landlady started for the kitchen. "The access is outside, but I keep a spare key in here."

As they climbed the exterior stairs to the apartment over the garage, Ruby glanced back. "Can I ask how she died?"

"We don't know yet," Jackson said. "Her body was found at the top of Skinner's Butte. Do you know why she was up there?"

"She liked looking at the city. It was one of her favorite places."

Was Zena new in town? "How long has she lived with you?"

"A couple of months." Ruby unlocked the door.

"How do you know she didn't come home?" Evans asked, following her inside.

Good question. Everyone was a suspect until they ruled them out.

"I would have heard her, and the apartment was still quiet this morning."

The studio had a single window overlooking the backyard, but otherwise was dark and minimalist. A couch, a bed, a card table with one chair, and a duffle bag on the floor by the kitchenette.

"I offered to take Zena to St. Vincent's to pick up whatever else she needed." Ruby gestured at the nearly barren room. "But she didn't seem to mind living like this."

"Do you know where her family is?"

19

Ruby pressed her lips together. "Zena was hiding from them and said I could never tell anyone she was here."

The back of Jackson's neck tightened. *Their first suspects.* "I need to know her parents' names and where to find them."

"I can't help you. The only reference Zena used was her employer, Starbucks." Ruby's voice cracked with emotion. "I usually require much more, but I took a chance on this girl. She was so sweet." The woman choked back more tears. "And so worried."

"You mean about her family finding her?" Jackson asked.

Ruby lowered her voice. "I think she might have left a cult of some kind. I overheard her fighting with her boyfriend, and she said something about being conned and never going back."

Jackson's whole spine tingled now. Cults could be vindictive against members who got out, and arguments with boyfriends often turned lethal too. "What's the boyfriend's name?"

"Dagen. But that's all I know." Ruby scowled. "He drives a loud, silver minivan, if that helps."

It might be enough. Jackson scribbled notes as fast as he could. "What does Dagen look like?"

"Kinda skinny with dark, wavy hair. And he wears a gray sweatshirt."

Like the kid at the scene that morning.

Evans cut in. "Do you know the name or location of the cult?"

"I'm sorry." Ruby shook her head. "I probed, but Zena didn't want to talk about it."

"What else can you tell us?" Jackson was eager to get online and see if Zena had social media pages that might be helpful.

"Not much."

"Can we look around?"

"Sure, but there's not much to see." Again, Ruby gestured around the bare-bones room.

Evans headed to the couch and pulled out the cushions. Jackson turned to the landlady again. "Did Zena have a cell phone?"

"Yeah. It was a new experience for her, and she had to ask for my help a few times." Ruby let out a chuckle. "I'm not exactly tech savvy, so it was odd to know more than a young woman."

"Do you have Zena's number?"

The landlady pulled a phone from the pocket of her sweatpants, then scrolled through her contacts. She turned the cell so Jackson could read the number. He keyed it into his own phone, then pressed the call button. It couldn't hurt to try. Maybe Zena's attacker had it and would be stupid enough to answer.

No such luck. The call went to a generic voicemail. The missing phone was another powerful reason he thought the girl had been assaulted in some way. Destroying or tossing the victim's phone was the smartest thing an assailant could do to thwart an investigation, and it was becoming all too common.

He looked up at Ruby. "Did Zena and Dagen fight a lot?"

"Not at first, but they had a couple of doozies in the last week or so."

"Do you know what about?"

She shook her head. "I heard the thing about being conned because I was outside, and Zena's voice is high-pitched and easy to understand. I started up the stairs to check on her, but the argument stopped."

Evans abruptly asked, "Can we see her rental application?"

"I'll go get it."

When Ruby was gone, Evans said, "Let's do a quick search, even though there's not much here."

Jackson picked up the duffle bag and set it on the bed, then started pulling out clothes. A pair of jeans, a couple T-shirts, and a heavy sweater. Under the clothes, he found several paperback novels about dragons, some jewelry, a ratty stuffed panda, a folder with drawings of dragons, and a picture of a young girl, likely Zena, at age ten or so with a woman who could be her mother. But no phone.

As the landlady hurried back in, breathing hard, Jackson's phone dinged, and he checked his texts. A message from the medical examiner: *TOD, 10-2 last night.* Jackson turned to Ruby. "When did you last see Zena?"

"Yesterday, around five, when she got home from her shift at Starbucks. We didn't talk though. I just saw her through the window, heading for the stairs."

"Did you see or hear her leave after that?"

"No. Sorry. I often go to bed before Zena goes out with her boyfriend."

"How did she meet him?"

"Maybe at Starbucks. She works at the one in the Safeway on Willamette Street."

"He's a co-worker?"

Ruby shook her head. "I don't know."

Jackson piled everything back into the duffle bag, then attached an evidence tag to it. He would submit the whole thing to the forensic lab for further examination. He looked up and noticed Evans scanning the rental application. "Anything interesting?"

"It's pretty skimpy." She side-stepped to stand beside him. "Move that, please."

Jackson knew why. He set Zena's bag by the door, then hustled back. Evans grabbed the mattress, but Jackson nudged her aside. "I'll do this part." At six-foot and two-hundred pounds, he could get the mattress higher. As he held it up, Evans looked around underneath. In the middle of the box springs was another folder. She snatched it out, and Jackson let the mattress fall back.

"What's in there?" he asked.

Evans pulled out a single document, sucked in a startled breath, then handed the stiff paper to him.

As Jackson scanned it, another surge of adrenaline coursed through his veins—like a bloodhound picking up a scent. A birth certificate for Kenna Slaney, born the same day as Zena Summers.

Chapter 4

Thursday, 6:30 p.m.

Jackson stopped at Full City and picked up two large Italian-roast coffees and a couple of turkey sandwiches. Back at the department, he passed Evans' cubicle.

She stood and followed him into his. "You bought me coffee, didn't you?"

"And a sandwich."

"You rock. I'm starving, and the taskforce meeting starts in twenty minutes." Evans perched on the corner of his desk and dug into her sandwich, talking as she chewed. Jackson loved that about her.

"I got online and searched for both of the victim's names and whatever cult she might be attached to."

"And?"

"A mixed bag." Evans took a swig of coffee. "Nothing on Kenna Slaney, but Zena has an Instagram account and posted about leaving a controlling situation. She didn't mention the cult or leader's name and didn't give much detail."

"Are they religious? Or paranoid isolationists?"

"I have no idea. We still have a lot of work to do." Evans gave a sly smile. "But I love digging up secrets."

Jackson smiled back. "Me too." He turned to his computer. "I'll check our database." He ate half his sandwich while the software loaded, then keyed in the name *Pearl Slaney*. The birth certificate they'd found listed Pearl as the mother, but the father's line was blank. Kenna had been born in Eugene, and he hoped to track down her mom, or any other relative.

Pearl Slaney's name came up in a traffic accident report from two years earlier. She'd rear-ended another car on West Eleventh Avenue near the Fred Meyer store. The report listed an address as on Louis Lane, but he couldn't visualize the area. He loaded Google Maps, keyed in the address, and brought the satellite view into focus—a big open area on the west end of town with a few scattered houses.

Evans, looking over his shoulder, said, "That's off Bailey Hill, across from the middle school. There's a huge private complex up there. I thought it was a church retreat."

"I wish we had time to check it out before the meeting." Jackson glanced at his computer clock. "But we have to head to the conference room now." He stuffed the rest of his sandwich in his shoulder bag and picked up his coffee. "Ready."

Evans hopped off the desk. "We could go up there afterward."

Jackson shook his head. "It'll be dark by then, and if there's a locked gate, we'll be wasting our time."

Evans didn't respond.

Jackson touched her shoulder. "Please don't go by yourself. We've got a cop killer on the loose, and someone from the cult may have killed Zena. It can wait until tomorrow."

"We'll see."

Jackson tensed, but he didn't push the issue. He sometimes took those kinds of risks himself. They headed downstairs to the big conference room.

"Another thing," Evans added. "Zena only opened her IG account five weeks ago. Her posts are all selfies of her doing everyday things, like seeing a movie, but her captions say stuff like *First time in a theater!* and *Great new experience!* She must have led a sheltered life."

"That seems typical of a cult. I wonder what inspired her to leave."

"We'll have to find out."

Jackson was skeptical. Cults were notoriously secretive, and members were often threatened with alienation or shaming to keep them from sharing the details of their inner workings with anyone on the outside. He wished the department had an undercover unit that could send someone inside.

Someone like Jamie Dallas.

He'd worked with the FBI agent twice, most recently to rescue a kidnapped woman, and Dallas' undercover skills made her perfect for this new case. He wondered how long it would take her to not only finesse her way inside but also learn the cult's secrets. Would the bureau even approve the assignment? They rarely got involved in local homicides, but cults—and the fraud they often committed—tended to cross state lines. It couldn't hurt to ask.

"Excuse me for a moment," Jackson said, stopping at the door to the conference room. "I have to make a quick call."

"To let Kera know you're not coming home anytime soon?" Evans smiled playfully.

Crap. He'd been so busy interviewing witnesses, he'd forgotten his family entirely. But Kera knew he had two active cases, and he would call Benjie later and tell him goodnight. "I'm calling Agent Dallas. We could use her skills again."

"As an insider. Of course." Evans nodded and headed into the meeting.

Jackson called the personal number Dallas had given him as they wrapped up their last case. It seemed like only a week ago. The line rang four times before she picked up. "Jackson. I'm surprised to hear from you. What's up?"

"We have a cult here in town that may have murdered a member who left. Any chance the bureau would let you come back and help us out?"

She laughed, a charming sound. "My leg is still healing from the gunshot wound from the last time."

He'd forgotten that. "Oh yeah. I shouldn't have asked."

"It's fine. I'm getting around pretty well now. What's the group?"

"We're still working on that. We just found the body this morning and learned about the cult a few hours ago."

"Send me what you have, and I'll call my boss and sound him out."

"Call him? Where are you?"

"Still in Flagstaff on vacation, but I'm supposed to head back to Phoenix soon."

"The weather is cooler here." Jackson chuckled at his feeble bribe. "No pressure. Really." Lammers walked by and signaled him. "I have to get to a meeting."

"Send me a dossier, and I'll get back to you."

"Thanks." Jackson clicked off, sensing Dallas wouldn't be interested. The case wasn't high profile or dangerous enough. Still, even without her, he could find the group's leader and investigate the old-school way, which had served him well for two decades. He hurried into the conference room, already full of detectives, feeling late for the second time that day.

"Now that we're all here," Lammers said, staring at him, "let's get rolling. We have a lot to cover." She turned her gaze to Schak. "Detective Schakowski, would you report on our interrogation, please. I'll update the board." The sergeant turned to one of the rolling whiteboards behind her.

Schak stood, looking tired. "Dominic Bulgar was mostly non-responsive, but his story is that Mitchell arrived at his house this morning around eight-thirty, presented him with a warrant for his arrest on a parole violation, then took him into custody. Bulgar claims the officer was shot as they neared the patrol unit."

Evans raised her hand. "Was the suspect in cuffs at the time?"

"No. Bulgar says he was cooperative"—Schak rolled his eyes—"so Mitchell didn't cuff him. He says he ran in panic after the gunshot, fearing he would be blamed."

"Bullshit," called Detective Dragoo, who was part of the unit that normally worked sex crimes.

"Bulgar did, in fact, surrender to patrol officers about twenty minutes after the shooting." Schak looked annoyed.

"He was afraid he'd get killed!" Dragoo was on a roll.

"That's not helpful," Lammers admonished. "Let Schak finish."

"There's not much else to report." Schak shifted on his feet. "Bulgar stuck to his story, and his hands tested negative for gun powder residue."

"He had twenty minutes to clean up," Dragoo argued. "And hide the gun."

"I'm not saying the guy is innocent," Schak blasted back. "I'm just summarizing the interrogation." He took a sip from his thermos. "We're tracking down his known associates and plan to pick up all of them." Schak sat back in his chair.

"There's more," Lammers said. "Right before the meeting, I got a call from our weapons expert in the crime lab. Berloni says the bullet came from a rifle, and the medical examiner confirmed that the shot was fired from a distance of at least twenty yards."

"Bulgar shot him from inside the house as he approached?" Jackson asked.

"Not likely." Detective Michael Quince stood, his movie-star face tense. "I interviewed his neighbors, and a reliable witness says she saw Officer Mitchell bring Bulgar out of the house. As they neared the patrol unit, she heard a gunshot and saw the officer go down. She thinks the sound came from the hill behind the house."

"Hills can echo in weird ways," Jackson commented.

"Bulgar must have known the arrest was coming," Schak added. "So one of his associates probably ran out the back and up the hill in time to take out Mitchell."

Quince, still on his feet, nodded. "I think so as well. Two of Bulgar's associates are affiliated with the Kings gang and are suspected of bringing in drugs from Central America."

Lammers updated the board with the witness information, then turned back. "Jackson, did you talk to Officer Mitchell's widow?"

"Not yet. I've been busy with the new case, and she hasn't returned my call."

Quince cut in. "According to texts on Mitchell's cell phone, his wife went to Portland to meet with a client and won't be home until about ten this evening."

Lammers grimaced. "We have to get this done." She glanced around the room. "Who wants to sit outside the Mitchell house tonight waiting for her?"

"I will." Evans raised a hand. "I'm usually up late anyway."

"Great. Thanks." The sergeant stepped away from the whiteboard. "Anybody have anything to add?"

The room was quiet.

"Dismissed," Lammers said. "Except for Jackson and Evans. I want an update on the new case."

Jackson moved to the front of the room and stayed on his feet, hoping to keep the meeting short.

"What have you got? Another homicide?" Lammers looked tired too.

"Most likely." Jackson wished they were in their own conference room.

Evans must have felt the same because she grabbed a second whiteboard and started a case summary as Jackson talked.

"The victim has no obvious lethal wounds, but she is banged up." An image of the body flashed in his memory, and Jackson's gut tightened. "She also recently changed her name from Kenna Slaney to Zena Summers. The woman she rents from says the girl was hiding from her family and maybe recently left a cult."

"What cult?"

"We don't know yet, but we're working on it."

"Talk with our liaison at the FBI," the sergeant suggested. "They might have a profile on the group. Cults often move from state to state to stay ahead of law enforcement when things get dicey."

Jackson nodded. "I've already asked the bureau for help." He paused, wondering what he'd left out.

Evans jumped in. "Zena also had a boyfriend named Dagen." She added his name and description to the board.

Another image flashed in Jackson's head. "A young male matching his description was near the scene this morning.

We have an ATL out for him and the other kid who was with him."

"Good. If you need help, pull in Schak." An odd look crossed Lammers' face. "And keep an eye on him, please."

Chapter 5

"Well?" Evans stared at him, her jacket and bag over her shoulder. "It's still early. Are we going?"

They stood in the foyer outside their cubicles. "Not now." Jackson was curious too, but visiting the Louis Lane address wasn't a priority. "We need more information about the cult first, and that address could be old or phony."

"What else have we got? At least it's a lead."

"We need to find the boyfriend. He's a better suspect."

"You're right. I'll search social media. You check the databases."

"Yes, ma'am."

Evans laughed. "Just keeping you on your toes."

Jackson wanted to pull her into his workspace and kiss her, but that would never happen. Even if they got together some day, they would have to remain professional at work. He had to break off with Kera first. A familiar pain seized his gut. He still hadn't made an appointment with his gastro surgeon yet either.

"What is it?" Evans asked.

"Nothing. Let's get to work." Jackson walked to his desk.

He opened the department's database—which contained the names of anyone who'd ever been mentioned in a police report—then keyed *Dagen* into the search field. Nothing. But the kid he'd seen on the butte that morning was probably too young to have a record and apparently had never been involved with Child Protective Services.

Next, Jackson accessed the national criminal database and got one hit. Dagen Johnson, a dark-skinned man, age 33, from Mississippi, who was currently incarcerated.

"I found him," Evans called from the other side of the wall. "Dagen's on Instagram, and his last name is Hammersmith." Evans was suddenly in his space. "Zena is one of his connections."

"Where do we locate him?"

"His parents are Mark and Lisha Hammersmith. Check our files."

Jackson searched for the dad first. He was more likely to have encountered the police. And he had. Ten years earlier, Mark Hammersmith had been charged with drunk driving and lost his license for a year. Jackson read the address out loud.

"See if it's still valid," Evans said.

Jackson was already accessing the county's property records. Lisha Hammersmith still owned the house, and he quickly found a phone number in the county's files. "Let's go chat with them." Jackson stood and grabbed his jacket. "Or maybe I should go alone. You have widow duty at ten o'clock."

"I've got almost two hours. I'm going."

Inside his car, Jackson wolfed the rest of his sandwich, then put on his headset and called his house phone. He'd kept the landline over the years so he could reach his daughter at home when she was younger. Now seventeen, she had a job and a cell phone, and he rarely saw her. But Benjie had come into his life, and he kept the line for the same reason. He hoped the boy was still awake.

Benjie's sweet little voice was suddenly in his ear. "Daddy?"

That beautiful word always made him smile. "Yep. Hi Benjie. How was your day?" Jackson pulled out of the department's lot and turned right.

"Great. We did clay animals in preschool, and I made a squirrel." He laughed. "It didn't turn out good, but I had fun."

"That's what matters." The boy was strangely mature and good natured, especially considering he'd witnessed his mother's murder, then hid under the house to save himself. Jackson had found him at the crime scene, and Benjie had clung to him. Their bond had been so intense he'd filed for custody after no other family members were located.

"How was your day?" Benjie asked.

"Busy and stressful." Jackson laughed. "I would have rather made clay animals."

"We have clay! We can do that when you get home." The boy was excited now.

Jackson heard Kera's voice in the background mentioning bedtime. "Maybe tomorrow. I'm still at work, and you have to go to bed."

"Okay. Be safe, Daddy."

Jackson's eyes felt warm and wet for the second time that day. What the hell was wrong with him? Had the counseling session made him overly emotional? He decided not to go back. Jackson had planned to have Benjie put Kera on the phone, but since she already knew he was working late, everything else he had to say could wait.

Five minutes later, after driving around to the other side of the golf course, Jackson arrived at the house on Roland Way. Evans waited on the sidewalk, a silhouette in the dark. Lights were on in the modest home, and TV images flashed through the thin curtains. An early model minivan sat in the driveway, parked off to one side. They started toward the front door.

"What's the plan?" Evans asked. "Are we taking the kid in for questioning?"

"That depends. If he's cooperative and has an alibi, we don't need to." Jackson knocked on the door.

Dagen was eighteen, so they could treat him like an adult. But if he was innocent, there was no need to traumatize him. He didn't have a juvenile record, so this might be his first encounter with police. Jackson knocked on the door.

A full minute passed before a voice came through a speaker. "Who are you? You look like cops."

Jackson glanced up at the security camera. "Detectives Jackson and Evans with the Eugene Police. We need to talk."

"About what?"

A little paranoid? "Dagen. Is he here?"

A long pause. Finally, a thin woman in her late forties opened the door a few inches. "Let me see your badges."

Jackson held out his and assumed Evans did the same. He didn't want to take his eyes off the opening, in case he needed to stick a foot into it.

"What do you want to speak to Dagen about?"

"A dead girl." Evans' tone was curt.

The woman gasped and closed the door.

"Shit." Jackson hadn't psyched himself for a confrontation.

Footsteps thumped across the house, followed by the muffled sound of voices.

Jackson pushed the door open and called out, "You're obstructing justice! I'm coming in."

"Going around back." Evans took off, rounding the corner of the house before he could respond.

It was the right move. As he hustled down the hall, a door slammed in the rear of the house. He ran toward the sound and ended up in a laundry room.

The mother stood in his way, shaking. "I tried to talk to him, but he was too scared."

Jackson pushed past her and charged out the back door. Evans and the young man both sprinted across the yard. He caught up to them as she slammed Dagen against the back fence. Jackson pulled out his cuffs and snapped them on the kid. Evans spun him around. "We just wanted to talk," she growled. "Now you're in real trouble."

They grabbed him by the elbows and walked him to the sidewalk. His mother came out the front, pleading. "Please don't arrest him. We'll answer your questions."

Jackson ignored her and turned to Evans. "I'll take him in. You have to notify Mitchell's wife."

"Oh crap. I'd forgotten." She headed for her car.

Jackson secured the suspect in the back of his sedan, then looked at the mother. "Where were you last night between ten p.m. and two a.m.?"

"Why are you asking?"

"You said you would answer questions, and I'm done being patient."

"I was home. I'm always home." A bitterness in her voice. "I have an autoimmune disease and chronic pain. It's all I can do to function."

He sympathized, but couldn't let that interfere with his job. "Is that your minivan?"

"It's Dagen's. I have a Honda CRV in the garage."

Jackson made a note of both. "What's your name? And your connection to Dagen?"

"Lisha Hammersmith, and he's my son."

"Same last name?"

"Yes."

"Where was *he* during those hours last night?"

A pause. "Dagen was here."

"Don't lie to me!"

"He was here when I went to bed at eleven." Her voice trembled.

Jackson didn't believe her. If Dagen had a cell phone, they would eventually be able to track his movements. That would take time though—first getting a judge to sign a subpoena, then waiting for the service provider to comply. Jackson hoped it wouldn't come to that. For now, he would get what he could out of the mother. "Do you know Zena Summers?"

"I've met her."

"Did she talk about her family? Or where she used to live?"

Lisha shook her head. "I just know she worked at Starbucks. I think that's where she and Dagen met."

"The girl is dead, possibly murdered. If your son didn't do it, then you need to help us." Jackson glanced at his car to check on him.

The mother was silent for a long time, then blurted, "Maybe Zena killed herself. Dagen said she talked about it recently."

Chapter 6

Evans sat in front of the Mitchell house, hoping the widow would come home soon. She wanted to check this off her list and hurry back to the department to participate in Dagen's interrogation. Jackson would wait for a while, but it was late, and he probably wanted to get it done and go home. *To Kera and the boys.* A thought that never failed to cause her pain. No matter who else she dated, Jackson was always there in the back of her brain—his dark good looks, his crooked smile, and the pale scar above his eye. Their one kiss lived in the center of her heart. But she had just met a terrific guy and hoped he would be the one to make her forget her feelings for Jackson.

Another ten minutes, and headlights came up the dark road. *Yes!* The car, a newer Genesis, pulled into the driveway, paused for the garage door to open, then rolled inside. Evans climbed out and headed for the entrance. The driver probably hadn't seen her sitting out here in her dark sedan. Evans rang the bell and didn't have to wait long. The woman who came to the door could have been a model—five-ten, with thick blonde hair, wide-set eyes, and pouty lips. Evans fought to suppress her feelings of inferiority. "Sloan Mitchell?"

"Yes." She was casually dressed in black slacks and a pale-blue silk blouse.

Evans wore nearly identical clothes, but she still felt dumpy. "Detective Evans, Eugene Police. My colleague has been trying to reach you."

"Oh no. What's wrong? My phone was off for most of the day."

"I'm afraid I have some bad news."

Sloan blinked hard. "It's about Darren, isn't it?"

"Yes. May I come in?"

The tall woman stepped back into a glass-and-tile foyer, her arms folded tight across her chest. "Just tell me. I've braced for this day."

All cop partners did. Evans decided to keep it simple. "Your husband was shot during an arrest. I'm so sorry, but he didn't survive."

Sloan covered her mouth as she cried quietly. After a moment, she choked out, "Wasn't he wearing his vest?"

"He was shot in the head."

"Goddamn." The widow suddenly strode into the next room and sunk into a plush sofa. Hands over her face, she took a moment to compose herself. When she looked up, her mascara was smeared. "Has it been on the news all day? Am I the last to know?"

"The department hasn't released any information. We wanted to inform you first."

"I appreciate that. I've been out of town consulting with clients." Sloan stared at her hands in her lap, then asked, "Did you catch the guy?"

"We have a suspect in custody, and we're looking for a second man." Evans wanted to give the woman some hope.

"Sergeant Lammers is handling the case personally, and we're confident we'll get the killer."

Sloan nodded and looked lost.

The next part was often harder for victims' families, but Evans pressed ahead. "Do you know anyone who would want your husband dead?"

"Besides all the criminals he put in jail?"

"Anyone recent or in particular?"

"Not that I know of. Darren didn't talk about his work much or mention specific names. He tried to spare me that."

Out of habit, Evans asked, "What about someone with a personal grudge?"

Sloan frowned. "I'm not sure what you mean."

"Someone in his personal life who harbored bad feelings." Evans was surprised she had to explain. "Maybe they were jealous or angry about past problems. An ex? Or a vengeful relative?"

Sloan shook her head. "Not that I know of."

"What about money? Did your husband owe an unpaid personal debt?"

The widow's jaw tightened. "You said he was shot in the line of duty. Why are you asking these questions?"

"I'm sorry. Force of habit."

The tall woman stood. "I have to call Darren's mother, then take a sleeping pill and lie down for a while."

"Of course." Evans thanked her and left, checking the clock on her way out. She might still make it in time for the interrogation.

Chapter 7

Thursday, 10:30 p.m.

While he waited for Evans—and let the suspect stew in his own anxiety—Jackson keyed his case notes into a file. The process helped him keep track of details and share daily updates with his team, which wasn't much of a crew this time. He needed help with interviews, so he texted Schak and asked him to meet in the small conference room the next morning. After sending the message, Jackson noticed he'd missed a text from Gunderson saying the autopsy was scheduled for the next day at one-thirty. Even with a limited taskforce, Jackson still planned to attend. He needed to see the victim's entire body, in case she had a lethal wound hidden under her clothes. Her missing fingertip bothered him even more now that he knew a little about Zena's history.

Eyes closed, Jackson leaned back in his chair, letting his mind drift. He was hoping for an inspiration or connection or to at least remember what he was forgetting. He tried to visualize the inner workings of the group Zena might have belonged to—and suddenly sat up. He'd forgotten to send the case sheet to Agent Dallas. He also didn't know the name of the cult yet, or if that piece of information was even true. He emailed a copy of his case report to Dallas anyway, then pushed out of his chair. Maybe Dagen could fill in some details.

As Jackson headed downstairs, he heard footsteps behind him and turned to see Evans. "About time," he teased.

She grinned, then handed him a small coffee as they entered the lower foyer. "In case we're here late."

"Thanks."

She stepped toward the narrow door on the left. "Let's hope Dagen is a momma's boy and tells us everything."

They both laughed.

Evans tapped a code into the security pad, then pushed open the door. Jackson followed her into the dark ten-foot-square room, bracing himself for the claustrophobia. The first few minutes were always bad, then he got used to it . . . for a while. If he stayed in the windowless space too long, the panic would hit him again.

"You can't just leave me sitting here like this." The kid banged his cuffed hands on the scarred wooden table.

"Standard procedure." Evans sat in the chair next to the wall, leaving Jackson closer to the exit. They'd done this together a few times.

"If you cooperate and don't seem like a risk to our safety, or yours, I'll uncuff you." Jackson nodded at the camera above the door. "For the record, this session is being recorded."

The kid blinked rapidly, his pale face glistening in an overhead light that shone straight down on him. The thick hoodie he wore had to be making him overheat. *But maybe not,* Jackson thought. Some people seemed immune to such things.

"I've never hurt anybody," Dagen whined. "This is all some kind of mistake."

"Then why did you run from us?"

"I was scared. And kinda high." He glanced around, not making eye contact. "This whole thing is freaking me out."

Marijuana had been legal in Oregon for five years, but not for anyone under eighteen. "How old are you, Dagen?"

"Almost nineteen."

"Were you and Zena having sex?"

"Yeah. Why?"

"Just establishing the nature of your relationship." Jackson leaned forward. "What were you doing at Skinner's Butte this morning?"

"What?" The kid looked confused. "I don't get up before noon, and I've never been hiking."

Jackson let it go. A lot of young men wore gray sweatshirts. "Where were you last night between ten p.m. and two a.m.?"

He blinked rapidly again, fear flashing in his eyes. "Please tell me what happened to Zena." Anguish in his voice.

Jackson wasn't impressed. Many killers regretted their moment of violence and often grieved for the victim. Jackson's instinct told him Zena's death had been intentional, but even if it had been an accident, he needed Dagen to be scared enough to admit his part. Jackson locked eyes on the kid. "She was likely killed, or at least left for dead, at the top of Skinner's Butte."

"You mean someone assaulted her?" He sounded upset.

That didn't mean anything either. This hellhole of a room brought that out in people. Jackson repeated his question. "Where were you last night between ten p.m. and two a.m.?"

"I was home for a while, then went to a friend's to eat pizza and play videos." Dagen sounded deadpan, like he was giving a practiced speech.

L.J. Sellers

"What friend? What time did you arrive? Walk us through your whole evening."

"Please take off the cuffs. I'd like something to drink."

Jackson uncuffed him, then Evans handed him a small bottle of water from her bag. Jackson suppressed a smile. She probably had snacks in there too.

"Do you have anything else?" Dagen whined. "I really hate water."

They ignored him.

After taking a tiny sip, Dagen said, "My friend, Zack Coulter, stopped by and picked me up—"

"What time?"

"Around ten."

That synched with what Lisha had said. "Go on."

"We bought a pizza at Dominos, then went to his place to play Manhunt."

A violent video game. "Do you spend a lot of time gaming?"

"Don't all kids?"

"What do you like about Manhunt?"

Dagen sensed the trap and backed off. "Uh, it's Zack who likes the game. That's why I go over there. I'd rather play Fortnite."

Sure. "Was anybody else in the house who could verify your presence?"

"No. Zack's roommate wasn't there."

"How long did you stay?"

"'Till about two in the morning, then I went home." Dagen glanced down as he mentioned the time.

Probably lying.

"That's not much of an alibi," Evans commented.

"I didn't know I would need one."

"We'll check it out, for sure." Jackson let that sink in. "When was the last time you saw Zena?"

More rapid blinking. "Not in a few days."

"Why not?"

"I think she was gonna break up with me."

"Why?"

Dagen shrugged. "Maybe she met someone else."

A diversion. "Do you have a reason to think that?"

"She was acting kind of distant."

"Were you fighting with her?"

"Not really."

"Did you ever raise your voice in her apartment?" Jackson wanted to trap him in a lie. That would give them leverage.

"Did her landlady tell you that?"

"Just answer the question."

"Okay. I yelled at Zena once because I thought she lied to me."

"About what?"

"I don't remember."

Evans cut in. "I don't believe it. Dishonesty in a relationship can be a dealbreaker. What was the fight about?"

Dagen shifted uncomfortably. "I probably said something stupid or accused her of seeing someone else. Guys do that stuff. It was no big deal."

"What about the bruise on her forearm?" Evans pressured. "Did you grab Zena and restrain her?"

"No." The kid tried hard not to look away from Evans, but he didn't succeed.

Jackson wanted to drill down through the timeline preceding her death. "Did you text with Zena last night?"

Dagen hesitated. "Why?"

"Those messages could help clear you." Jackson held out Dagen's phone, which he'd confiscated earlier, but hadn't looked at. Technically, Oregon law considered it a personal computer, and he needed a subpoena. "Do we have your permission to open your phone and check your messages?"

A wave of panic. "No."

What was he hiding?

"Do you have texts between you and Zena from last night?" Evans asked again. "You might as well tell us. We have access to Zena's phone records."

The kid let out a sigh. "I messaged Zena earlier and asked if she wanted to hang. She said she had other plans, and I accused her of ghosting me for another guy."

Jackson cut back in. "So you were jealous and angry with her." They had to get Zena's phone records too.

"I already admitted that, but it doesn't mean I killed her."

Jackson decided to switch it up and see what else they could learn before their suspect melted down or asked for a lawyer. "What do you know about Zena's family?"

He shrugged. "She was upset with her mother and didn't want her in her life. That's about all Zena would say."

"Any mention of her father? Or siblings?"

"No."

"Do you know anything about a cult?"

Dagen scowled. "You mean the place she lived before?"

"Did she talk about it?" Evans pressed.

"Not really. And she never called it a cult. She just said she escaped a controlling situation."

Nobody in a cult ever thought they were in a cult. Jackson remembered what the landlady had overheard. "What about her feeling like she'd been conned?" Jackson asked. "What did Zena mean by that?"

"I don't know. I never heard her say it."

Had Ruby misunderstood? Or had Zena been talking to someone else? Maybe even on the phone. "What else did she say about the situation? Did she mention a place? Or the name of someone in charge?"

"I heard her mumble something about Jove once when she was having technical trouble with her phone, which she was quite obsessed with."

"J-O-V-E?" Jackson wanted to be sure.

Dagen shrugged. "How would I know?" The kid suddenly slumped in his chair. "I'm really tired and hungry."

Jackson ignored him and mixed it up again. "Did Zena tell you how she lost part of her finger?"

Dagen sat back up, seeming eager to cast blame somewhere else. "She said it was a punishment, then wouldn't talk about it any more. She seemed to get scared every time her past came up."

Oh shit. The cult sounded dangerous, and Jackson vowed to find it and help the other members. But he still thought Dagen was their best suspect. According to statistics, when a woman was murdered, the killer was usually a man she'd been intimate with.

Chapter 8

Friday, Oct. 2, 6:45 a.m.

Dallas got up and dressed quickly. If Cameron woke, he'd want her to come back to bed, and she wouldn't be able to say no. But she was eager to get back to work. She'd been idle for three days in Flagstaff, and restlessness had set in. Her boyfriend wouldn't be happy about her taking another assignment so soon, but she wasn't ready to give up undercover work.

Dallas started a pot of coffee, then went out for an easy walk/run, forcing herself to ignore the pain and put full weight on her wounded leg. She needed it back to full strength as quickly as possible, especially if she got the green light to return to Eugene for another gig. With her earbuds in place, she called her boss.

"Special Agent Radner."

She visualized him behind his desk in the corner office of the Phoenix bureau. "Good morning. It's Dallas."

"How's the leg?"

"Better. In fact, I'd like to take a new undercover assignment." She rounded the corner and had to zip her jacket against the wind.

"I'll see what we've got."

"I have one in mind already." She hesitated, wondering how best to frame the request. "The Eugene Police Department needs me to infiltrate a cult that's physically abusing its members and might have committed murder."

"That could take months."

"Or not. You know I work fast. I can use the same fake ID from our last case because the groups are in completely different worlds."

"You sure about that?"

"Yes. The cult is run by Jove Goddard, aka James Grabski, and it's based on a fear of technology. So they're not online." Jackson had sent a file the night before, followed later by a text with the first name *Jove*. She'd accessed the bureau's database and eventually found him. "His group, or message actually, is called Simple Path, and it may be part of a larger movement of neo-Luddites."

"You say the leader murdered someone?"

"Possibly. The victim is an ex-member who'd recently left the cult and changed her name because she was afraid of them finding her." Dallas stopped to rest her inflamed leg. *Was she really ready for this?*

"Who would be your contact?"

"Detective Jackson with the EPD."

"I'll trust your judgment and let you take this, but I need you back here in six weeks." A pause. "And have the EPD file a formal request for our help."

"I will. Thanks." She started walking again, vowing to ignore the pain and do her job.

"Also, send me a dossier and let me know what else you need for support. Eugene's field office doesn't have many resources."

"I've still got the handgun that fits in the hidden panel of my purse, so I'm good."

Radner made a noise in his throat. "Is the cult armed?"

"Most neo-Luddites are passive, but some splinter groups are run by paranoid types. I suspect Jove Goddard is the latter." Dallas turned and headed back. "He chose that name, so he clearly has a god complex. The combination could be dangerous."

"Be careful."

"Always."

"Yeah, right." Radner chuckled.

Cameron wasn't amused. "Why does it have to be you? The FBI has other undercover specialists." He set his coffee down on the counter and started to pace. "You're still not recovered from your last assignment." Cam spun around, his handsome face lined with worry. "Which you promised would not be dangerous."

"The original assignment wasn't, but then it morphed into something else."

"Which could happen this time too."

"This is my job. You knew that when—" Dallas stopped. Actually, they'd met in high school when they'd taken theater classes together and fallen in love. After graduation, Dallas had wanted to get out of Flagstaff and away from her drug-and-alcohol-addicted parents, but Cameron had stayed. They'd hooked up again when she'd come home for her father's funeral a year ago. Now he was pressing her to give up the undercover work and settle down with him. At times, she was tempted.

"You're never gonna give this up, are you?" Sadness filled his voice.

"Of course I will. I'm almost thirty. Most of these gigs require a UC who's young and hot."

"You'll always be hot."

Dallas smiled. She *was* blessed with a great face and body, and she tried to use it for the good of others by bringing down criminal organizations from the inside. "This time it's personal. I feel like I owe Jackson a favor." He'd helped her save two kidnapped women, one who'd been imprisoned for years.

Dallas also wanted the challenge of infiltrating the cult. Her last assignment hadn't required a 24/7 immersion, just outings as bait for a rapist. "I can get this done in a couple of weeks, I promise. Then I'll come straight back here and take the rest of my vacation days."

"I know I can't talk you out of it." Cameron tried to smile. "And I'm not stupid enough to give you an ultimatum. So come back to bed for another round of mind-blowing sex to hold me over."

"Let me book a flight to Eugene first."

Chapter 9

Friday, 6:00 a.m.

Jackson woke to the quiet beeping of his phone alarm. He reached under his pillow and quickly shut it off, hoping not to wake Kera. She rolled over, patted his chest, then dozed back off. Still groggy after only four hours of sleep, he forced himself to get out of bed and move through his morning routine: shower, prednisone, and work clothes. The medication kept his retroperitoneal fibrosis in check.

Still functioning in semi-darkness, he retrieved his service weapon from its locked safe and hurried to the kitchen. While coffee brewed, he made toast and mentally mapped out the tasks he had to accomplish that day. The list was overwhelming. Jackson took a deep breath. *One thing at a time.* His new mantra. Being a father to two young boys and maintaining an older home while working as a homicide detective regularly forced him into survival mode. The first few days of an investigation were always the worst, but they had a solid suspect already. The time crush and lack of sleep would be over soon.

"Hey, Dad." Katie shuffled into the kitchen, yawning. "You're hitting the coffee early."

"I've got a new case. What are you doing up?"

"I'm volunteering with a cleanup crew for Amazon Creek. Homeless people treated it like a dump this summer." Katie rolled her eyes. "I'm supposed to say *unhoused*, but I just can't do it. Too weird."

"I'm with you on that." Jackson handed her a piece of toast. "I'm proud of the work you do."

"Just trying to be a good citizen."

Jackson poured a cup of coffee. "Want some?"

"Just half, so I can add a lot of milk. Your coffee is so strong, it's like snorting cocaine." She laughed. "Not that I know what that's like."

Jackson tried not to think about the year she'd spent partying. "What else is new with you?" He poured her a half cup, then put the rest into a thermos.

"Straight up honest?" Her expression shifted.

"Always." Jackson sat down at the table, prepared to spend as much time as this needed. The taskforce meeting was hours away.

Katie sat down too. "I don't want to move into the new place with you and Kera."

He'd dreaded this moment since she left home the first time. "Because of Kera?"

"No. She's great." Katie sipped her coffee. "This is my home where I grew up, and it feels normal to be here, for now. But when I move out, it should be into my own place. You know what I mean?"

"I think I do." Jackson tried to keep his expression neutral, but his heart hurt. "Still, you haven't finished school, and you're not a legal adult yet, and—"

Katie reached over and squeezed his arm. "I'll be fine. A group of us from work are talking about getting a place together. Plus, I plan to finish my senior year online. I'm so done with sitting in class and dealing with all the juvenile bullshit."

It would all be okay. The other half of his new mantra. Maybe he should tell her what he'd been thinking. "We haven't signed the rental agreement yet. If you strongly object, I would reconsider." Maybe this was his out. *No.* He needed more than a temporary solution.

"I don't object. You and Kera and the boys need a bigger space, and I—"

Benjie padded into the room. "You're having breakfast without me?"

"Nope." Jackson got up and hugged the boy. "I'll make you toast and eggs right now."

Two hours later, a tray of coffee containers in hand, Jackson entered the detectives' conference room, a smaller space than the main meeting area downstairs. Surprised Evans wasn't already there, he unloaded the to-go cups and took a seat at the end of the table. A moment later, a whiteboard rolled in, with Evans pushing from behind.

"I grabbed the one I started yesterday." She shook her head. "Not that we have much to work with."

"We'll get there. Schak is joining the team, and I'm thinking of asking McCray to help out too."

"Great idea. I miss the old guy."

Jackson did too. He and Ed had been partners in the unit for a decade, then McCray had retired a few years ago. But golf hadn't been enough for him, and he'd formed a cold-case team with other retired detectives and sometimes did freelance work for Jackson's taskforce. "I'll probably ask him to do some surveillance."

"On Dagen?"

"Yeah." They'd released the young man around midnight and told him to be available for more questioning.

"Who's Dagen? And what kind of hippie name is that?" Schak hustled into the room, surprisingly quick for his barrel-shaped body.

"The victim's boyfriend and our only suspect." Jackson gestured at the coffee he'd brought.

Schak sat down. "No pastries?"

"He's staying on Tracey's good side," Evans teased. "Or maybe your wife bribed him."

"Whatever. I already hit Voodoo Doughnuts on the way in." Schak smirked, then got serious. "What have we got?"

"An eighteen-year-old girl found at the top of Skinner's Butte." Jackson glanced at his notes. "She died sometime between ten p.m. and two a.m., Wednesday night. No obvious lethal trauma to her body, but there's a gash on her neck, likely made from a branch or rock."

"Maybe she got high and fell down. Or overdosed." Schak liked to present counterpoints to keep them from moving too quickly into group think.

"That's certainly a possibility." Jackson nodded. "But she's also missing part of a finger."

"The perp cut if off?" Schak seemed taken aback.

"It's an old injury. When we interrogated her boyfriend last night, he told us Zena said the amputation was a punishment."

"That's freaking weird."

Evans added the detail to the board, then pivoted back. "The victim's landlady says Zena is hiding from her family and may have recently left a cult."

"The most dangerous time for women is when they leave." Schak's tone was gravely serious.

Evans nodded. "That's why we're treating this like a homicide."

"The autopsy is this afternoon," Jackson added. "We may not get a full determination, but the pathologist will likely have an educated guess."

"What do you need me to handle?" Schak asked.

"A subpoena for the victim's phone records."

Schak glanced at the board. "Her name is Zena Summers? That sounds made up."

"It is." Evans pointed to another detail. "We found a birth certificate that indicates she was born Kenna Slaney and recently changed her name."

"That fits with hiding from a cult or whoever abused her." Schak shook his head. "Do we know anything about the cult?"

Jackson summarized the text he'd received from Dallas that morning. "The leader is a man named Jove Goddard, aka James Grabski. He's part of an anti-technology movement known as neo-Luddites. His particular splinter group is called Simple Path, and we might know where it is."

Evans cut in. "Jackson and I are headed out there after this meeting." She bounced on her feet.

Where did she get her energy? Jackson glanced at Schak. "Any update on Officer Mitchell's case?"

"You didn't get Lammers' email?"

Jackson hadn't checked his work messages yet. "No. What's up?"

Schak sipped his coffee. "Dominic Bulgar has two associates who are deep into the Kings drug gang."

"But they haven't picked them up yet?"

Schak shook his head. "They're in Portland. You really should read your email."

Jackson knew Schak was teasing, but he had a flash of embarrassment for not doing his job. He needed to make a to-do list and not let his family situation sidetrack him. He also needed to delegate more. "Evans, will you run a background check on Lisha Hammersmith?"

She snapped her head toward him. "What's your thinking?"

"My gut tells me she's hiding something, other than protecting her son."

"Yeah, I got that vibe too."

"What else you got for me?" Schak asked.

Jackson recited the address on South Louis Street. "Call the county and find out who owns the property—and anything else about it that seems important. In fact, do that first. We might need the information right away."

"Text me the address."

Jackson almost laughed. Schak had resisted texting for years, claiming his thumbs were too big for the keys. But he'd come to appreciate the easy—and less personal—access to information.

"Anything else?" Jackson looked around, but his teammates shook their heads. "Let's get back to work then."

Chapter 10

Jackson turned left off Bailey Hill and drove slowly up the narrow lane. Scattered homes sat back from the road, surrounded by grassy fields and clusters of trees. Most of the houses had been built in the sixties or earlier, but their acreage probably made them quite valuable now. A half-mile later, the lane ended at a gate with a tall brick wall stretching into the landscape on both sides. Frustration filled his belly. When they'd checked the area on Google Maps the night before, the wall hadn't been visible. Obviously, the image was several years old.

He parked in front of the gate and waited for Evans to pull up behind him. They climbed out in unison and stared at the stone barrier, which was eight feet tall. The two-panel gate was made of metal and designed to retract on both sides. A security post with a keypad sat off to the left.

"Goddard is big on privacy." Evans shook her head. "This structure wasn't on the aerial images I checked out."

"I know. It makes me wonder what else is back there and how we would get in, even with a subpoena."

Evans gave a sly smile. "The SWAT unit's armored truck could get through." She was the only woman on the special team, and she'd trained for six months to get strong enough to pass the physical.

"Let's hope it doesn't come to that." Jackson pulled out his phone, snapped a picture of the barriers, and sent it to Dallas with the caption: *This is why we need you.* "Agent Dallas is on her way. She texted this morning with the information about Jove Goddard."

Evans turned to him, her expression wary. "What kind of egomaniac names himself Goddard?"

"I'm worried too." Jackson stepped toward the security box, looking for a buzzer. He found it and pressed. Several minutes passed.

"They have a camera." Evans pointed at a small device on top of the gate. "They likely know we're police officers and will ignore us."

Jackson pressed the buzzer again. After a few more minutes, a deep soothing voice came through the speaker. "Who are you? And why are you here?"

"Detectives Jackson and Evans, Eugene Police." A brief sense of *deja vu* fluttered in his brain. "Who are *you*?" Jackson demanded.

"Jove Goddard. Why are you here?"

"We need to ask about—" Jackson hesitated, unsure of which name to use—"Kenna Slaney."

A pause. "Why?" His voice was less soothing now.

"She's dead."

A longer pause. "I'm sorry to hear that, but I still don't know why you're here."

Jackson's patience waned. "Her mother Pearl lives here, and we need to speak with her."

"I can convey your message. Now please leave."

"That's not how it works." Jackson let his irritation be known. "This is a police investigation, and if you don't let us talk to Pearl, we'll come back with a subpoena and question everyone."

"That's an empty threat, but I'll tell Pearl you want to see her." A pause. "Harmony is love." The speaker clicked, and the founder's voice was gone.

"Do we wait?" Evans asked. "He didn't say he would send her out."

"We'll give it a minute." Jackson wasn't optimistic.

Evans snorted. "For someone who preaches anti-technology, he sure uses electronics to keep people out."

Jackson texted Schak: *Anything on the property yet?*

"Let's see how far the wall goes." Evans took off through the trees.

"Wait!" Jackson shouted.

She stopped and turned back, her expression surprised. "What? I wasn't going far."

An image of her being hit by a sniper had flashed in his brain, and his heart raced. "Let's be careful. We don't know what's out there or how big this compound is."

She gave him a side eye. "You mean like booby traps?"

"Or guard dogs."

She jogged back and stood on the road. "This property is within the city limits, and there's a Christian college not far from here. I'm sure some of the students have wandered over." Evans smiled. "And survived."

"Fair point." Jackson felt embarrassed for the second time that morning. "Still, I'd feel better if we were wearing tactical gear."

"Let's push for a subpoena too."

Jackson's phone dinged, and he checked his messages. Schak had texted: *13 acres owned by nonprofit Simple Path, which also owns several other lots in area. Goddard is founder.*

Jackson relayed the information to Evans. "The bastard doesn't even pay property taxes on all this." He pressed the buzzer again.

Goddard responded more quickly this time. "Pearl doesn't want to talk to you."

"Tell her we'll be back."

Chapter 11

Friday, 1:25 p.m.

The elevator doors opened, and Jackson stepped into a dark, narrow hallway. The basement of the old hospital housed the county morgue. A few doors down, he stepped into the stainless-steel room, blinking at the sudden brightness. Rich Gunderson, the medical examiner, had just arrived as well, and they both pulled on hair coverings, gloves, and masks.

"Thank god this is my last year on the job," Gunderson muttered. "I'm too old to be working nights and weekends anymore."

"I know how you feel." Jackson's body sympathized, but his psyche still loved the chase.

"You don't have to be here." The pathologist, who conducted the autopsies, walked over from his workstation. "Go home and rest, Rich. Jackson and I can handle this." Rudolph Konrad was Jackson's age, but his blond hair and chubby cheeks made him look younger.

"I'm already here," Gunderson grumbled. "I had to come in and prep the body, remember? And there are a few things from the scene I want to point out." He strode toward the wall of stainless-steel drawers. "Let's get rolling."

The two men worked together to move the corpse from cold storage onto a narrow table under the intense lights in the middle of the room. The medical examiner peeled back the white fabric covering her body, while the pathologist checked his tool tray.

Jackson stepped up to the table and gave Zena's naked body a once over. He felt less voyeuristic about it now than he had in his first years on the job, but it still made him uncomfortable. Her arms and legs had been out in the sun recently, but her midsection and breasts were pale. She didn't have any broken skin or blood that he could see. The bruise on her wrist stood out even with her tan.

Konrad often started a meticulous skin search at the victim's feet, but instead, he probed her neck wound with a gloved hand. "I'm doing this for you, Jackson," he said, his voice deadpan. "I know you just want the highlights."

"It's all I have time for." Jackson started to explain, then stopped. Both men knew about Officer Mitchell's murder and the department-wide search for his killer. They'd conducted an autopsy on him the day before.

Konrad used a small flashlight to examine a piece of debris he'd removed. "Some kind of leaf. This gash was likely made by a sharp branch scraping her neck shortly before she died. But it's not the cause of death."

"She did lose a lot of blood," the ME countered. "The ground under her was soaked."

"It's possible the bleeding hastened her demise." The pathologist shifted his gloved hands to the dead girl's scalp. "This abrasion on her head was a bleeder too. She could have been struck by a heavy weapon, such as a flashlight. Or maybe she hit her head on a rock when she fell. Once I get the particulate debris under a microscope, I'll know more."

Jackson glanced at the medical examiner. "What about her backside? Does she have any wounds?"

"Nothing new, but there's an ugly scar from years ago. Probably made with something hot, like a curling iron."

Konrad cleared his throat. "That's my job to determine." After a moment, he added, "I x-rayed the corpse earlier, and she has an old break on her collarbone too. Plus, there's a recent bruise on her forearm."

A rush of rage burned in Jackson's chest. "It seems safe to assume she'd been abused."

"It's never safe to assume anything," the pathologist corrected.

Jackson regretted his choice of words. Nothing about this case was certain . . . yet.

"She could've been accident prone, which would explain her fall on the rocky slope." Konrad nodded at Jackson. "You're probably correct about the abuse, but I don't see anything that could be lethal. I'll know more when I get her open, but I can't determine the cause of death until the toxicology report comes back."

Which could take days, Jackson thought. "Can we rush that please? She recently left a cult where other children may be suffering abuse as well. I need every bit of evidence I can gather to get a search warrant."

The pathologist nodded, then continued to examine the victim's skin, mentioning a mole on her left shoulder. He switched to her other arm, then picked up a magnifying lens and examined a small area on the upper part. "An injection site, most likely from a vaccine."

They'd all had vaccines and boosters recently.

Konrad searched her chest area, mentioning "generally healthy tissue." When he reached her abdomen, he stopped and pressed. "Hmm." The pathologist took a half step toward

Jackson, then pushed gloved fingers into the victim's vagina, while pressing on her belly again with his other hand.

Uh oh. Jackson had seen this before.

"This girl was pregnant," Konrad announced. "And I'd guess the fetus is about three months along."

Chapter 12

Five years earlier

Kenna spread mortar on a brick, then carefully placed it on the row she'd just completed. With the edge of the trowel, she wiped off the excess mud and repeated the process until she had another full row. She grabbed the level and checked her work in several places, then made a small adjustment. She often had to correct the work of the girl who did the early shift on this side of the wall, but Aisha was small and uncoordinated, so Kenna didn't mind. She'd already completed five rows in this section of the wall this morning and felt proud of her progress. But her arms were tired, and the sun was getting hot. It had to be close to quitting time.

Kenna checked her watch. Twelve more minutes. At age thirteen, she was required to work on it for three hours every morning while school was out for the summer. She'd hated the chore at first—so messy and difficult to keep the bricks level, or *plumb*, as Jove called it. But she'd gotten better and faster and had come to enjoy the accomplishment. It felt good to contribute to their community and help keep everyone safe. She finished the next row, cleaned off her tools, and walked home.

Inside the cozy house, she grabbed her homemade backpack and filled it with a sandwich, a water bottle, and the Dragonfire book she was reading. The rest of the day was hers to do whatever she wanted—within the compound, of course. School started next week, so this was her last free afternoon, and she hoped to slip out without her mother seeing her. Not that she planned to do anything wrong, she just liked the sense of nobody knowing exactly where she was—a rare occasion in her limited world.

"Where are you headed?" her mother called from the kitchen.

Dang. "Out to the woods to read by the creek."

"Will you make time for your brother this afternoon?" Her mother's sad eyes were hard to turn away from. "Then harvest more tomatoes and cucumbers, please."

"Sure. See you later." Kenna hurried out before her mom made other requests. Pearl worked evenings as a waitress at a nearby restaurant and spent her days meditating, studying the teachings, and helping Jove, so Kenna did most of the cooking and cleaning in their tiny home. She didn't mind too much. It gave her something to do besides walk in the woods and read. Life in the compound was simple and safe, but boring—unless she screwed up. Kenna longed to be part of the outside world, even if it was dangerous and bad for her mind.

Later, as she was picking ripe tomatoes, eating the little sungolds as she went along, she spotted Uncle Craig near the main greenhouse. He wasn't really her uncle, but many of the adults in the community were referred to as aunt or uncle. Jove wanted everyone to feel like family. Craig glanced around to see if anyone was watching, so Kenna quickly turned away. She squatted near her basket and watched him out of the corner of her eye. Uncle Craig made a beeline for the rocky side of the forest behind the compound.

Where was he going? Adults almost never went out there, and the boys who used to play in the woods now spent their afternoons working on the wall.

Kenna got up and ran between rows of corn to the far end of the garden. She knew it was wrong to follow Craig, but she couldn't help it. He was up to something, and she had to know. Kenna skipped across the narrow field, hoping to look casual, then darted behind a tree. Her heart pounded and her stomach tightened into knots. If she were caught spying, she would be shamed or shunned for a while. But if Craig were caught violating the no-tech rule, his punishment would be worse.

Kenna had been outside the compound a few times with her mother—to see a dentist, to take swimming lessons one summer, and shop for clothes sometimes. While out in the real world, she had read every sign and listened to every conversation, making mental notes for later. There was so much she didn't know, so much she wanted to learn. Most of all, she wanted a cell phone. Everyone on the outside had them and seemed quite engrossed. She knew they connected to the internet, because Jove preached about the dangers of "being plugged in." But Kenna was skeptical. The "electric sheep," as Jove called outsiders, seemed pretty happy.

She hurried after Craig, sticking to the patches of soft grass to quiet her footsteps and hiding behind trees and blackberry clusters. Craig kept going until he reached the back of the property, then ducked behind a boulder. A wire fence with a barbed topper lined the compound up here, and beyond the fence sat a massive structure that held a city water reserve. Or so she'd heard.

Kenna ran for an oak tree and began to climb. If she could get high enough, she would be able to see what Craig was doing. She hoped it wasn't a sex thing. Men's naked bodies were kinda gross. It probably wasn't though. Jove taught that sex was healthy, so Uncle Craig had no reason to hide for that. Climbing the tree was such joy, Kenna almost didn't care about Craig for a moment. But when she was high enough, she straddled a thick limb and scooted forward until she could spot him.

He had a phone!

Kenna's pulse throbbed in her throat. She was both scared for him and excited for herself. Tonight was movie night for adults, and Craig always attended. While he was distracted, she would sneak into his house, find his hiding place, and see what the big deal was all about.

After her mother left for work, Kenna made chicken and rice for dinner, then worked on a thousand-piece puzzle with her younger brother, Ben. The poor kid had disabilities, but he was good at matching colors and shapes. Around eight, she put Ben to bed early. "Hey, kiddo. You can look at your books for a while, but don't get up. I'll check on you later."

"Goodnight, Kenna."

"Night." She kissed his forehead and left the small room they shared. After waiting a few minutes, she changed into a dark shirt and went outside. The temperature had dropped, and she shivered as she crossed the gravel lane in front of their house. She missed summer already and dreaded the cold bleakness of the coming winter. What if she took Craig's phone and kept it? He couldn't report it or confront anyone without getting into trouble himself. Then she would have something to distract herself with during the dark months.

Stealing was wrong, she knew. But if Craig wasn't supposed to have the phone because it was dangerous, maybe she would be doing him a favor. Women were more self-disciplined than men, so she probably wouldn't be ruined by the lure of technology like Uncle Craig would.

Jove had been sent to warn the world, men especially, about the dangers of the internet, but it was too late, he'd realized. Yet he was still trying to save those he could.

Kenna had second thoughts and stopped next to a chicken coop. What if having the phone filled her with crazy thoughts? People would notice, and she would be shamed. Would her mother be kicked out? Pearl would be traumatized if that happened, but Kenna rather liked the idea. She started down the path to Craig's house. She had a vague memory of his wife and their new baby, but she couldn't remember what had happened to them.

As she'd expected, his back door wasn't locked. It was a mostly unspoken Path rule, a way of trusting each other. A stab of guilt made Kenna hesitate again. But now that she was here, moments from getting her hands on a phone, she couldn't turn back. She glanced around, noting the house was shaped exactly like theirs. But Craig's space was cluttered with clothes on the couch and dirty dishes on the coffee table. This wouldn't be easy.

If the phone were hers, where would she hide it?

Not in the living room. Kenna hurried into the adjacent kitchen. Maybe in a coffee can or a package that looked like noodles. No, that was what she would do, because she cooked. Craig's stove was piled with used paper plates, which meant he probably ate a lot of sandwiches. She backtracked to the hall and entered a small bedroom. It would be in here somewhere. A secret hiding place.

She started her search carefully, putting things back exactly as she found them. But it was too time consuming, and she began to leave clothes and papers wherever they fell. In the overall mess, Craig would never notice. Kenna checked under the dresser drawers too, in case the phone was taped to the bottom. Nope. She checked the vent in the floor, sticking her arm down into the dusty darkness. Not there either. Under his pillow? Another strike out.

Not knowing how much time had passed, Kenna's anxiety mounted. She had to get out, maybe try again later. As she started for the door, her foot slammed into a toolbox, partially covered by a pair of jeans. She pushed the pants off and searched through a collection of screwdrivers, pliers, and other greasy tools. In a bottom corner, wrapped in a red cloth, she found it. A small black cell phone.

Heart pounding, she tucked the forbidden device into her pocket. She had no idea how to use it, but she would figure it out. Kenna shut the toolbox, put the jeans back over the top, and rushed into the hall.

As she bolted toward the back door, Craig and Jove walked into the living room.

Oh no! No, no, no!

"Stop!" Jove yelled.

Kenna froze. Running was pointless—unless she could make it all the way out of the compound and never look back. But she couldn't do that. Her little brother needed her. She turned and broke into sobs. "I'm so sorry!"

Later, the three of them sat in her own living room, waiting for her mother to return. The silence made Kenna's heart want to explode, but Jove had forbidden any talking. Kenna tried to read, but couldn't concentrate. Poor Uncle Craig just sat there, sighing.

When Pearl walked in, her face crumbled. "What's wrong? Is it Ben?"

"It's Kenna." Jove's tone was strangely soft now, unlike earlier. "She stole Craig's phone."

Her mother gasped, dropped her purse on the floor, and came to sit by Kenna.

"Do not comfort her," Jove instructed. "This is a serious infraction. I'm thinking of kicking all three of you out of the Path."

Pearl spun toward Craig. "Why do you have a phone? Why did you let Kenna see it?"

Jove held up a hand, his face tight and no longer handsome. "Not now." He stared hard at Pearl. "If you want to stay, are you prepared to face the consequences?"

"What are they?" Her mother's lips trembled.

Kenna felt horrible. *What had she done?* "Don't punish my mother, please."

"Quiet!" Jove stood and locked eyes on Pearl. "Are you prepared? Yes or no?"

"Yes," her mother whispered.

Jove turned back to Uncle Craig. "Let's get it done."

Kenna jumped up, instinct telling her to run, but she stepped in front of her mother instead. "No! This is my fault!"

Jove abruptly grabbed her, stuffed a rag into her mouth, and shoved her against the kitchen counter. Kenna tried to scream, but gagged on the cloth. Jove's powerful arms encircled her shoulders, holding her in place. Kenna turned back toward her mother, pleading with her eyes for help, but Pearl looked away.

Uncle Craig, standing on the other side of the counter, started to cry.

What was happening? Kenna's heart pounded so hard she could hear it. Her mother stepped up, grabbed Kenna's left arm, and held it down on the counter. In one swift motion, Craig grabbed a cleaver and cut off the tip of her pinkie finger. The searing pain and gushing blood shocked her. For a moment, Kenna blacked out. When she opened her eyes, Pearl was wrapping her finger and murmuring, "You'll be okay, baby girl."

Jove leaned in behind her and whispered, "If you steal or touch a cell phone again, you'll lose your whole hand."

Chapter 13

Friday, Oct. 2, 3:05 p.m.

Jackson pulled into the Safeway on Eighteenth Avenue, parked and hurried inside. The aroma of fresh coffee gave him an instant lift. Even if he didn't learn anything from Zena's co-workers, he would at least get a decent cup of brew to power him through his growing task list. Two Starbucks employees bustled around a narrow space at the front of the store. Jackson walked past the single customer waiting in line and stepped up to the counter person, a tall young girl with kinky hair whose nametag said *Sav*.

Short for Savannah? He introduced himself, then added, "I know you're busy, but I need a few minutes of your time."

The girl stared, as if in shock. "Right here, right now?"

"Is there somewhere else we could have this conversation?"

The two round tables off to the side were occupied, and the little kiosk didn't have a back room.

"Not really."

"Okay, then. Here we go. Do you know Zena Summers?"

"Hey!" A man's voice called from behind. "I was here first."

Jackson turned. "Eugene Police, and this is important." He hoped the guy had the good sense to back down, but a lot of assholes now felt empowered to be their true selves, and it made everyone's jobs harder. He pivoted back to the barista. "Zena?"

"Yeah. She works here. Or she did. She missed her shift this morning, and they called me in."

"Do you know anything about her life?"

"You mean like her boyfriend?"

"Yes."

"His name is Dagen. So cool. Like dragon. I only met him once, and he seemed nice."

"What did Zena say about him? Did she ever mention anger or abuse?"

The tall girl's eyes went wide. "Uh, no. Is she okay?"

"We'll get to that. Did Zena ever talk about where she used to live? Or about leaving a controlling situation?"

"No. But she did say she wanted to become a social worker and help children." Sav bit her lip, which was pierced by a small silver ring. Another one adorned her eyebrow. "Why are you asking?"

Jackson didn't want to mention Zena's death until he'd talked to the other employees. "Did anyone else here know Zena better?"

Sav spun around and yelled, "Kai! Get up here."

At the back counter, a slender young woman with pink hair muttered something, then walked carefully toward them, carrying coffee drinks. She set them on the end of the counter. "What?"

"This cop wants to ask you about Zena."

"Is she in trouble?"

Jackson shook his head. "Did you hear from her yesterday?"

"No."

"Did she tell you about the cult she just left?"

Pink-Hair's eyes went wide. "She said her mother was kinda crazy, but she didn't mention a cult."

"She ever mention being scared of someone?"

A blank stare.

"Or talk about what happened to the end of her finger?"

"No, and it would have been rude to ask."

"Did she use drugs?"

"She mentioned smoking pot once, but said she hated it."

That didn't mean much. "What about opioids?"

"I seriously doubt it. She looks healthy."

Zena had apparently been a private person, so the next question was likely a waste of time too. "Did she mention her pregnancy? Or who the father was?" Another longshot question.

Both baristas looked stunned. "No way!" Pink-Hair made an explosive gesture with both hands. "Mind blown."

Something sparked in Sav's eyes, and she blinked back tears. "Zena is missing or dead, isn't she?"

"Yes. I'm sorry. If you think of anything that could help me figure out what happened to her, here's my number." Jackson handed a business card to the tall girl. "Leave this at the counter for other employees to see."

He started to leave, but Pink-Hair suddenly called out, "Zena mentioned a journal and making notes for a book she wanted to write. Maybe there's information in there."

Why hadn't they found it in her apartment? Jackson vowed to go back and do another search.

In his car, Jackson headed for the department, feeling like he'd forgotten something. A few minutes later, it hit him. He and Kera were supposed to sign the lease on the rental this afternoon at four. He'd meant to talk with her about canceling the appointment, maybe the whole idea, but then he'd been assigned this case, and she'd been served with a custody suit. *Oh hell.* The property management company was downtown as well, so he turned on Fifteenth and tried to decide how to handle the situation.

He strode into the office, feeling late, and looked around for Kera. She wasn't in the lobby. He mentioned their appointment to the receptionist and asked if Kera had already gone back to the signing office. She hadn't. Jackson waited five minutes, then called her. A few minutes later, he texted as well. No response. Suddenly worried, he got up and paced. Five minutes later, he cancelled their session and walked out, his emotions a mess. He felt relieved that the moving-in-together plan was on hold, but worried that Kera had been in an accident. Or worse. This was so unlike her.

Yet he had to push all of that aside for now. He had a meeting scheduled with the taskforce, including McCray and Dallas, who both needed a full briefing. At this point, Zena Summers had been dead for thirty-six hours, and they were getting nowhere. The window of opportunity to solve this case was closing.

Chapter 14

Friday, 5:30 p.m.

As Jackson trudged up the back steps into the department, a familiar pain tugged at his gut. He ignored it and called a nearby deli to order pizza and sandwiches. His team would be working late again, and the least he could do was feed them. He didn't know what Dallas liked to eat, but if her plane was late, she wouldn't make the meeting anyway. He hoped she would. They had to work out communication details before she went undercover in the cult—if she succeeded in getting inside.

At his desk, he updated and printed his case file notes, then called his daughter. Katie surprised him by answering. "Hey, Dad. You working late?"

"Yeah. I've got new recruits to brief and new leads to follow. Are you home?"

"And I picked up Benjie from pre-school. We're good."

"Is Kera home?"

"No. Micah's not here either. What's going on?"

Jackson sighed. "Kera got some bad news yesterday. Her ex is filing for custody of Micah."

"That sucks." Katie was quiet for a moment. "Did she and Micah go into hiding?"

"I don't know where she is, and I'm a little worried."

"If she shows up, I'll tell her to call you."

"Thanks." A surge of pride and joy warmed his heart. After a wild year of drinking, while grieving for her mother, his daughter had developed into a mature young adult who he counted on to help with Benjie, and food prep, and too many other things. "I appreciate all you do for our family, Katie."

"I love that boy as much as you do."

Jackson smiled. "Give him a hug for me. I'll try to be home, or at least call, before his bedtime."

After ending the call, Jackson's thoughts shifted back to Kera. Now he felt less worried about her safety and more concerned for her emotional health. He hoped she was meeting with her ex and trying to work something out.

Time to compartmentalize and put his family away for now. Jackson picked up the case copies and crossed the wide hall into the conference room. After a few minutes alone, his old friend scooted through the door. "McCray!"

Still slender in his trademark corduroy pants, the retired detective moved like a cat, sliding into a chair in one smooth motion. "Hey, partner. I hear things are crazy around here."

Jackson had left him a brief message earlier, but McCray was still connected to the department's gossip network. Jackson nodded. "More than usual. Darren Mitchell's murder has us all worried and spread thin. Thanks for joining us."

"Happy to." His tan face glowed with fresh sunshine.

"Did you get out golfing this afternoon?"

"Of course. The warm sunny days are fading fast."

Evans waltzed into the room. "McCray!" She put an arm around his shoulders and squeezed. "So good to see you and work with you again. We need the help." She picked up a copy of Jackson's notes.

"I love surveillance," McCray said. "A chance to do something meaningful."

"What about the cold cases?" Jackson asked.

"When we finally solve one, yes, but the payoff is slow." McCray grinned. "This gig will get me out of the house at night, which keeps me from feeling like an old man."

They all turned as Schak trudged in. "McCray, old man. Nice to have you back." Schak sat across from Jackson. "Tell me you ordered pizza."

"Sandwiches." He'd let the pizza be a surprise.

"Bleh! I eat those every day."

Evans laughed. "And pizza every chance you get."

"So?"

Jackson was enjoying the camaraderie, but they had work to do. As he passed out the case notes, a food delivery person hustled in and set the bags and boxes on the table.

Schak grinned, gave Jackson a heart-love gesture, then helped himself to a slice of pepperoni. Jackson tipped the delivery person, and she scooted back out. Schak tore off a huge bite, gave it a few chews, then washed it down with whatever was in his thermos, spilling some on his white shirt.

Evans laughed. "I think you're actually devolving. Almost to the point of being feral."

Schak gave her the finger and took another bite.

Jackson's phone beeped, and he checked his messages. Dallas had texted: *Landed. Too late for meeting?*

He gestured for the others to eat, then called Dallas. "We're just getting started, so I'll put you on speaker and save you the hassle of coming in."

"Great."

Jackson cranked up the volume and set his phone in the middle of the table. "I think you've met everyone here, except McCray, our freelancer." Jackson glanced around at his team. "Agent Jamie Dallas is joining us via teleconference."

Evans leaned in. "Hey, Dallas. Good to have you on board."

"Always happy to visit Eugene. Quirkiest place I've ever been."

Schak grunted. "Dangerous too."

"Let's get started." Jackson grabbed a sandwich. "The most significant development is a mention of Zena's journal, which we didn't find in her room." He'd already sent Dallas the notes, and he hoped she was up to speed.

Evans wrote *journal* on the whiteboard. "We need to ask her landlady about it. Or maybe the killer took it."

"There may not be a perp," Jackson countered. "Zena has no lethal wounds. The pathologist conceded that the gash in her neck might have bled enough to be a contributing factor, but it's not the main cause."

"What does he think happened?" Evans asked.

"An overdose of drugs or alcohol. Konrad is waiting for the toxicology report to issue a finding."

"So the autopsy was no help?" Evans frowned.

"Except, we now know Zena was three months pregnant. Once we have the baby's DNA, we might be able to determine the father."

Schak cut in. "That's such a longshot."

Dallas' voice resonated from his cell phone. "The fetus' DNA could be critical. Sexual promiscuity and abuse are common in cults. Most egomaniacs feel sexually entitled."

Schak shrugged. "If we find enough evidence, I'll write a subpoena for it. That seems to be my default mode here."

Jackson caught his eye. "Thanks."

Evans took up the narrative. "We need to determine when Zena actually left the cult." Evans paced, sounding re-energized. "What if she was raped by someone out there? And he's trying to cover up his crime?"

McCray held up a hand. "Wait a minute. I'm lost here. What cult?"

Jackson updated him with what little they knew. "It's why I've asked the FBI for help. Dallas is an undercover specialist who plans to infiltrate the group and learn what she can from the inside."

"That sounds somewhat extreme for a victim who may have simply overdosed." McCray looked sheepish. "I mean, unless there's something else going on."

Jackson didn't blame him for thinking that. "The dead girl was also missing a fingertip, which she reportedly said was a punishment. The cult is worth investigating on its own."

"Absolutely," Dallas added. "Child abuse is also common in isolated communities. They're usually hiding for a reason."

"Then I'm glad you're on board, Dallas." McCray nodded at the phone. "Good luck to you."

"What else?" Jackson glanced at his notes. "Let's not forget the boyfriend." He looked at Evans. "Did you follow up on his alibi?"

"Of course. But I couldn't corroborate it. His friend, Zack Coulter, says Dagen left around one in the morning, not two. So Dagen lied to us and had time to meet Zena at the butte before she died."

Jackson looked over at Schak. "Any update on Zena's phone records?"

"Judge Cranston signed the subpoena, and I sent it to the service provider, but I don't expect anything until Monday.

I'll be on the phone first thing that morning pushing for the data."

"See if you can get a subpoena for Dagen's phone records too. Lying to us about his alibi may be all the evidence you need."

"Will do." Schak nodded.

McCray leaned in. "What do you need from me?"

"To keep an eye on the boyfriend, Dagen Hammersmith."

"Am I watching for anything in particular?"

"I'm mostly worried he's a flight risk, or that he might try to destroy evidence." Jackson wasn't sure what else to give him at this point. "Except for cult members, we don't have another suspect."

McCray stared at the board. "What about the victim's family?"

"Her mother, Pearl Slaney, lives in the compound and won't talk to us."

"Once I get inside, I'll check her out." Dallas paused for a rumbling sound in the background. "Anybody else you want me to focus on? Besides Jove Goddard, the narcissist in charge?" She let out a sarcastic laugh. "Most people with a god-complex aren't insecure enough to name themselves that way."

"But they are insecure." Evans shook her head. "The combination of feeling inferior yet entitled is disgusting and dangerous."

"I'll get something on him," Dallas vowed. A car door slammed. "I'm at my B&B now and need to get the key and unpack. Anything else I should know?"

"We're here for you," Jackson said. "Call any of us, any time, day or night, if you need help. I'll text the list of numbers."

"I'll send out info as I access it," Dallas said. "The group is anti-technology, so I'll have to be careful about using the burner phone I hope to smuggle in. You'll likely get texts from me in the middle of the night." Dallas sounded confident, despite the risk. "And they may not have computers for me to hack, so I'll send photos instead of files."

"Whatever you can do," Jackson said. "Just be safe. We don't know if they have weapons."

Dallas laughed. "They always have weapons, but so do I."

They were all quiet for a moment.

"Okay, I'm out."

Jackson picked up his sandwich, but didn't feel hungry anymore. "Let's wrap up. I'll go talk to Ruby, the landlady, again and ask about the journal, as well as pinpoint exactly when Zena showed up here in town."

Schak tapped the table. "Hey, I did learn that Zena started her cellular service on August third, if that helps. Getting a phone was probably one of the first things she did."

Jackson nodded. "If she had the money."

Evans snapped her fingers. "According to her ID and birth certificate, Zena was born on July twenty-sixth. I'll bet she left the compound on her eighteenth birthday."

"Makes sense." Jackson had another idea. "We also need to track down an ex-cult member if we can. So in your spare time—"

Footsteps pounded in the hall, then Sergeant Lammers burst through the door. "We've had another officer shooting."

Chapter 15

Around the same time

Dallas paced the B&B she'd rented online while sitting in the airport that afternoon, relieved that her leg felt almost normal. She needed to plan her strategy, but she felt restless and wanted to get out. Hanging around this weird mobile home was a waste of time. She'd never been a TV watcher—except for medical dramas and sci-fi movies—and she was tired of reading her limited material about Simple Path.

The bureau knew very little about the group, except that it had been around for nearly twenty years and before that James Grabski had once hosted a radio program in central California. Analysts estimated its membership to be around a hundred people, including those who lived both inside and outside the compound, but it was just a guess. Goddard didn't seem to actively or personally recruit members, so his followers likely did. The biggest mystery was where their funding came from, especially without an internet presence.

Dallas decided to go check out the property before it got completely dark. She loaded a small backpack with stakeout necessities—snacks, water, a black knit cap, and binoculars—then put on running shoes. She would have to stop at a St. Vincent's tomorrow and buy some used clothing.

Her luggage was still full of the sexy dresses she'd worn as bait on her last assignment.

Outside, she climbed into the beat-up Toyota offered with the rental for an additional $75 a day. Perfect for her needs. She planned to pick up a bunch of crap at the second-hand store and load it into the backseat, so she could say she was homeless and sleeping in her car. Unless her fieldwork took her in another direction. She'd learned to improvise and take on whatever personality would get the job done. Undercover was the ultimate acting gig, and she loved it.

Dallas loaded the address into her phone and pulled out, noting the compound was only three miles away. Eugene was such a pretty town, and everything was so accessible. People who lived here considered it to be a moderate-sized city with a major university. But they'd never been to Phoenix, a metropolis that covered 14,600 square miles. She both loved and hated the Valley of the Sn, and she got the hell out whenever she could.

Seven minutes later, she neared the end of Louis Lane. Dallas pulled off the road under some trees next to a gravel driveway, grateful the rental car was dark green. In the twilight, passersby might not even see it. She grabbed the backpack and jogged the rest of the way, staying off the road and out of sight as much as possible.

She'd studied aerial images of the area, then had to mentally modify them after Jackson's update. Intrigued by the wall, she wanted to see how far it went. Completely encircling thirteen acres with brick or concrete would have been insanely expensive, unless they did the work themselves and bought the materials at discount. She hoped to discover the wall only covered the area visible from the entrance road. If she ran out of daylight this evening, she would come back at dawn to approach from the opposite side, assuming she could find an access through the adjacent properties.

To avoid the camera at the gate, Dallas took off to the right, cutting through shrubs and clusters of trees until she came to the wall. At least eight feet tall and visually intimidating, but it was easily scalable with the right equipment. She shook her head at the thought. Her goal was to get invited inside as a member, as quickly as possible, and find out everything she could by almost any means. The FBI had rules, but UC agents were given a lot of leeway. As long as she produced results, her boss never asked probing questions.

She jogged parallel to the structure, keeping a reasonable distance away just to be safe. The cost of buying security cameras to cover this undeveloped area of wild grasses, Scotch broom, and scrubby trees seemed prohibitive. After a hundred yards or so, the brick wall curved south toward the top of the hill, then after another hundred yards, abruptly ended. Beyond that, a five-foot wire fence continued for the length of a football field, then disappeared into a massive blackberry bramble. She could have easily climbed over the fence, but that wasn't her mission this evening. She had wanted to assess the potential access points, and now she knew that a tactical unit on foot, or in an all-terrain vehicle, could enter here.

With her binoculars, she gazed into the protected acreage. A massive garden bordered this chunk of western boundary. Much of its bounty had been harvested, but the squash and pumpkins were still growing. A giant greenhouse stood at one end of the garden, and on the other end, she spotted a row of small cottages. The setup reminded her of a prepper/doomsday community she'd infiltrated outside of Redding, California.

The sun was dropping in the sky, so she headed back, intending to find out how far the wall extended in the other direction. As she neared the entrance road, she heard rumbling and ducked behind a tree to keep watch. The gate clanged open, and a small white truck exited. The driver, a young man, glanced briefly in her direction, then accelerated quickly down the road.

Dallas abandoned her original plan and sprinted toward her rental car, dodging shrubs and trees as she ran. The quickest way inside the compound to learn its secrets was to make a personal connection with a member. Young men were particularly vulnerable to her charms.

She followed the truck to downtown Eugene, where it parked behind a tavern called Blair Alley in the Whitaker neighborhood. Dallas squeezed her rental into a corner spot, pulled her hair out of the ponytail, and hurried after the guy. Since she'd only gotten a brief and distant look at him, she was afraid she wouldn't recognize him in a dark bar full of other men his age. Still, he'd seemed quite attractive, with a strong jaw and chin and big, wide-set eyes—a man who would stand out.

Inside the crowded venue, 80s music pulsed from a DJ's sound system, and people, mostly women, danced shoulder to shoulder in a small space near the stage. The rest of the noise came from the twenty or so pinball machines on the other side of the room. Crowds of young men swarmed the area, and the overall sound was deafening.

Dallas went straight to the bar counter, thinking her target was likely buying a drink. He was. She spotted him at the end, near a big cooler of help-yourself water. His lavender T-shirt and thick bronzy hair confirmed him as the guy she'd seen earlier. Definitely her type, which would make seducing him easier. Too bad she was wearing all black. But her jeans and T-shirt fit tightly, and she'd already caught the attention of several men.

Dallas eased in next to him, letting her body brush against his. He casually turned his head.

"Oh, sorry." Dallas gave him a half smile. Normally, she would have given him the full hundred watts, but for her character, she wanted to seem vulnerable, maybe a little needy.

The moment he saw her, his expression brightened. "Well, hello."

"Hi." She waited a moment. "I'm Amber." She still had the same fake ID from her last gig. Her long, blonde hair was natural this time, but she'd cut and dyed it in the past for other assignments. Whatever it took.

"Argus. But I go by Augie."

She gave a small chuckle. "We sound like a comedy team."

"What?"

"Amber and Augie." *Wrong approach?*

"I don't know those guys, but I like comedy."

Pretty and not too bright. Her favorite target. "Me too. But I haven't had many laughs lately."

"No? How come?"

"Oh, just bad luck and cursed technology." Dallas shook her head. "Excuse me, I need to get some water." She stepped to the nearby card table and filled a plastic cup. When she turned back, Augie was staring at her.

"Can I buy you a real drink?"

"Uh, okay. That would be nice." She sipped the water. "What are you drinking?"

"A house beer. It's called honey-something."

"I'll try it." She loved microbrews and had been delighted to discover that Cameron operated a brewery in Flagstaff. Dallas shut down the thought. No thinking about her boyfriend. She was Amber, a down-on-her-luck, gullible type who needed some kind of salvation.

While Augie ordered a tap special, she studied him. Five-eleven, muscular, and young. He didn't look old enough to be in the bar. The lavender shirt meant he was either color-blind or cocky enough to not care what other men thought of him. Also, he lived in a gated compound run by a cult leader who was probably abusive. Dallas bet herself that this guy had been raised by a single mom who was in love with Jove Goddard.

Augie handed her a beer, then lifted his for a toast. "To better times for both of us."

"I'll drink to that." *He was vulnerable. This would be too easy.* "Sounds like you're having a hard time too."

"Yeah, but I can't talk about it."

Yet. Dallas softly stroked his bare arm. "I'm sorry. Are you homeless too?"

He looked startled. "No. Why? Are you?"

"For the moment." Dallas sighed. "My boyfriend cheated on me, then kicked me out. And I'm kinda new to this area, so I didn't exactly have a backup plan."

"That's harsh."

"For sure. But I'll work it out." Dallas took a long drink of her beer. *Too sweet but not bad.*

He started to say something, then stopped. "You're not sleeping outside, are you?"

"I have my car." *Oh hell.* She hadn't bought the necessary props yet. It was too soon to go all in with him anyway. She had to play a bit coy. Make him chase her. Dallas changed the subject. "So what's your life about? Are you a student?"

"Not at the moment. I work at a garden store."

"That sounds nice." She'd created two options for herself and decided to go with the second. "I'm a freelance massage therapist." She would set up a website or FB page tonight but wasn't worried. As a neo-Luddite, Augie wasn't likely to check her out online. Did he even have a cell phone?

"I could use a massage." He blushed. "And pay for it, of course."

"That would be cool, but I don't have anywhere to set up my table." Or an actual table. Dallas decided to call it for the night.

"Maybe at my place." Augie reached over and squeezed both her shoulders.

An aggressive move she hated. "Okay. Let's set up a time tomorrow. Should we meet here?"

Disappointment obvious on his face. Poor guy had thought he was getting laid.

"Uh, yeah. I work until three. But the store is real close, so I can be here soon after."

Dallas downed another long pull of beer, then pushed the glass away. "I have to go. There's a place I like to park and sleep, but I have to get there before someone else does." She leaned in and kissed his cheek, letting her breasts touch him lightly. "I'll see you tomorrow." She hurried out before he could react.

Chapter 16

Friday evening

Jackson pulled up in front of the funky house on Olive Street, relieved to see lights on. Driving around to talk to people who weren't home was such a time waste, but calling in advance could send them scurrying, so they didn't have to answer questions. Now that another cop had been shot, he felt pressured to wrap up this case quickly and assist with the more-critical investigation.

Ruby Bannon took her time getting to the door, but she greeted him warmly.

"Sorry to bother you, especially this late, but I need to ask a few more questions." Jackson buttoned his jacket against the cool night air.

"No bother. Come on in."

He stepped inside, spotted the cats on the couch, and declined her offer to sit. "Zena's co-worker mentioned that she kept a journal. Do you know anything about it?"

"I saw her writing in a notebook once outside on the steps. She said she wanted to publish her story someday."

Was that what Goddard feared? Having the cult's secrets widely exposed? "We didn't find the journal in her room or her duffle bag. Do you know where it is?"

"Are you suggesting I took it?" Ruby looked offended.

"Not at all. I thought maybe she'd given it to you for safekeeping."

Ruby shook her head. "I would've told you."

Maybe Zena's assailant had taken it. *Crap.* But he still had other leads to follow. "Zena's boyfriend, Dagen, thinks she was dating someone else. Did you ever see her with another young man?"

"No. Just Dagen."

"That conversation you overheard when Zena mentioned *getting conned* and *not going back.* Are you sure it was with Dagen?"

Ruby pressed her lips together, seeming to recall a memory. "I saw Dagen out front earlier, so I'm pretty sure."

A dead end. "What day did Zena move in?"

A pause. "Around the first of August."

Jackson calculated the timeline. Zena had left the cult on, or soon after, July 26, moved into Ruby's studio around August 1, then secured phone service a few days later. Fast work for a girl who'd lived a sheltered life. Her mother must have given her money. "Can I see the apartment again?"

"Of course." Ruby went to fetch the key. "I'll let you go up by yourself. I don't like to go outside at night unless I have to."

"I won't be long." Jackson hurried back out, rounded the garage, and climbed the stairs, his scar tissue complaining with every step.

Ruby had left the apartment unchanged, like they'd asked her to. Jackson strode to the small bathroom in the back. He'd glanced in there the day before, but he hadn't seen anything to search and hadn't yet been convinced her death was foul play. This time, he looked in the waste basket, empty except for facial tissue, then opened the small medicine cabinet and found a bottle of aspirin and toothpaste. Her toothbrush lay in the sink, and a nearby narrow shelf held a hairbrush, blow dryer, and a few makeup items. He pulled back the shower curtain and spotted only a shampoo bottle and a razor. No drug paraphernalia. No journal. Jackson tapped the walls for possible hiding places, then scooted out of the closet-sized room.

The kitchenette consisted of a countertop with a hot plate and sink, a mini-fridge, and a single set of upper and lower cabinets. Zena owned a few dishes, a plastic pitcher, and a scratched saucepan. He had checked the refrigerator yesterday, and nothing had changed. Several small containers of yogurt, some grapes, and plastic-wrapped cheese slices. The whole vibe of her minimalist-and-poor space depressed him. He'd never lived in a place like this, having moved from his parents' home at the age of twenty into another house with his new wife. Jackson started to close the fridge, then noticed the shoe-box sized freezer compartment. He pulled it open, finding only a package of frozen blueberries. On impulse, he pushed them aside to check the back.

A plastic sandwich bag with a thin stack of cash inside.

What the heck? Without removing the bills, he fanned them like cards and counted about $275. An odd place to keep money, but there wasn't enough to alarm him. Maybe she just didn't trust banks. Paranoid, cultish people were like that. As he stuffed the plastic-wrapped cash into an evidence bag, he noticed something small and square under the bills— a sealed packet with the label blacked out by a sharpie. *Was it some kind of drug?* That seemed both unusual and unlikely. Nothing so far indicated Zena had used any kind of illegal substances. He would submit the evidence to the lab for testing and see what they reported.

Sprinkles of rain landed on his face as he pounded down the stairs. *Finally!* They'd had a long dry summer, and the moisture was long overdue. After returning the key to Ruby, he drove toward his home. The plan was to continue working, but he could search online from his personal laptop. His objective was to find someone who'd left the cult and might have insider information. He also wanted to conduct more background research into Dagen and his mother. She'd acted rather paranoid, which was typical of people who were drawn to conspiracy theories and the cults that formed around them. Maybe she and her son knew more about Simple Path than they were telling. They might even be members or ex-members who'd been assigned to keep an eye on Zena.

When he reached his house, Kera's car wasn't in the driveway. Another cacophony of emotions overwhelmed him—worry, relief, guilt, and frustration. He didn't need a personal distraction right now. He needed to wrap up Zena's case so he could help locate and prosecute Officer Mitchell's assassin, who was now likely targeting other cops.

As he walked into the kitchen, Benjie ran and jumped into Jackson's arms. "Daddy!"

He hugged the boy tightly and kissed his forehead, loving the scent of baby shampoo and apple juice, with a hint of sweet sweat. "Hey, Benjie. How was your day?"

"Better now!" The boy shimmied down. "Come see what I made."

"Give me a sec." Jackson removed his service weapon and set it on top of the fridge. If he didn't end up going back out, he would lock it away as usual.

In the living room, Benjie pointed excitedly to a truck he'd built with multi-colored, specific-shaped Legos. Jackson had been buying him specialty kits because the boy had gotten bored with the limitations of the basic ones. "Wow! Great job." He squatted down and examined the handiwork. "Does it have moving parts?"

"Yes!" Benjie's eyes lit up as he demonstrated how the front loader worked. Jackson held up his hand for a high-five. "Well done."

His daughter hurried into the room. "He was supposed to be taking a bath."

Jackson stood, wanting a hug from Katie too. But now that she was a young woman, he waited for her to initiate personal contact. She gave him a fist bump and a bright smile. "Glad you made it home for bedtime. Now I don't have to listen to him whine about you not being here."

Benjie glared. "I don't whine. I express my disappointment."

Jackson couldn't help but laugh. "Go take your bath, then we'll read a story." After the boy hustled out, Jackson looked at Katie. "Have you heard from Kera?"

His daughter handed him a slip of paper. "I found a note she left for you."

All Kera had written was: *Call me when you have a moment to focus.*

"At least I know she's okay and hasn't been kidnapped."

"Only you would say that."

"Me and everyone else who investigates violent crime." Jackson stepped out onto the back deck for privacy to make the call. Kera picked up immediately. "Wade, my love. I'm so sorry for missing the signing and for making you worry, but I didn't want to distract you with my problems."

"A brief text would have been helpful."

"I sent one."

"I didn't get it." *Had he missed it somehow?* "That doesn't matter now. What's going on? Is this about Daniel's custody filing?"

"Of course. I was so rattled, I couldn't think straight. So I called Daniel, and he's willing to negotiate for joint custody."

"I think that's good news." Jackson paced the patio, wishing he had a beer, a rare feeling for him.

"It is good. All I have right now is a guardianship." Kera paused. "I never filed for full custody because it's expensive, and we had to pay for Benjie's legal fees, plus the attorney for that other lawsuit."

Guilt triumphed in the battle for Jackson's emotions. "I remember. But where are you? Why aren't you home?"

"I'm sorry, but when I'm around you and your intense masculinity and huge kind heart, I can't make objective decisions." A longer pause. "I need some space to figure out what's best for me and Micah."

Jackson's lungs contracted in a sharp intake of breath. *Need some space* was code for *I want to leave you.* He was surprised by how much it hurt and unsure of what she meant, but he assumed they weren't moving in together.

Kera continued. "Daniel offered a proposal that I'm considering. He wants to buy or rent a duplex so we can live side by side and share Micah on a daily basis."

Jackson was too stunned to respond. What did she mean by *we*? He had no intention of moving in next door to Kera's ex.

"I'm seriously thinking about it because it would be great for Micah and would save me the expense and trauma of a custody battle I might lose."

She had made up her mind. He could tell. "Will you call the rental company and tell them we're not taking the house?"

"Okay. We probably didn't need that much space anyway."

None of it mattered in the moment. He was wounded, but strangely giddy too, as though he'd lost a limb freeing himself from a trap. Out of habit, he shifted into tactical mode. "I'll line up other care providers for Benjie so you can do what you need to do without any obligations here."

"Hey, I'm just reconsidering our living conditions, not walking out of your lives." Kera sounded upset.

"But you've left us before." *Ten months,* Jackson thought. "You'll always put your family first. As you should." *Might as well say the bottom line out loud.* "We both know you plan to accept Daniel's proposal and move out."

During the long silence that followed, Jackson's phone beeped. "I have to get back to work." He ended the call and gulped down two long breaths. They would get through this. He just wanted it to be over quickly. Another long breath, then he checked his phone. He'd missed a call from McCray.

Chapter 17

Friday evening

Schak slumped into his desk chair, then took long slow breaths. *Another officer shot!* Darren Mitchell, the first victim, had been a good friend. They'd bowled together on the department's league team, and their wives had arranged for occasional dinners together. His death felt overwhelming, and Schak vacillated between paralyzing grief and uncontrollable anger. Now Dale Perkins had been shot in his own driveway—but his Kevlar vest had saved him. The shooter had somehow disappeared without being spotted. Who was next? This job had always been dangerous, but now it felt like a suicide mission.

Schak had been on the fence about retiring for years, but now it seemed like the better option. He could stay engaged part-time with cold cases and occasional gig work the way McCray did. But first, he had to find, arrest, and help convict the cop killer.

Schak sat up straighter, pulled out his flask, and took a sip of bourbon. *Just one.* The heat gave him comfort, and he was able to bring his mind into focus. Rather than believe the officers had been chosen at random—which put everyone in the department at risk—he wanted to find a link between the men. Or at least figure out who'd killed his friend Darren. The second shooting could have been a copycat crime.

Schak opened the last three reports each officer had filed and scanned through them, looking for any overlap. Reading reports was boring, but it was better than writing up subpoenas. Jackson had sidelined him on the other case, so he had time to work this one. Maybe he would solve it and end his career with a big win.

Realizing he'd zoned out for the last five minutes, Schak reread a few sections. An unusual name popped off the page. *Jorio Radovick.* He'd been listed as a known associate in the drug-dealing case Mitchell had been pursuing and as a potential suspect in a gun-running operation from El Salvador, a case Perkins had on the back burner.

Schak keyed Radovick's name into the search bar and waited for his file to load. The thug had only one conviction for assault, but he'd been picked up and questioned in numerous crimes. Once more couldn't hurt. But first he had to find a current address. He accessed the county's property files and came up with a location in West Eugene. Schak stood and stretched, hoping to shake off the sleepies.

"You heading out?" Quince called from the door of his workspace.

"Yeah, but I'm not done for the day." Schak grabbed his jacket and satchel. "I want to check out a suspect in the shootings. Jorio Radovick. He's mentioned in recent reports by Mitchell and Perkins."

"No kidding? Have you told Lammers?"

"Not yet. I just found the link, and it's a longshot."

"You were going alone?" Quince looked surprised. "I'll join you, and we'll call Lammers on the way. We may need backup."

"Good plan." Schak hadn't wanted to ask for help, but he was relieved to have it.

Quince insisted on taking his sedan, so Schak notified their sergeant while his partner drove. Lammers said she would send a patrol unit to be on standby. "Good work, Schak."

"Thanks." He ended the call, feeling more confident.

"You okay?" Quince asked.

"Yeah. Why?"

"You seem quiet. Tired."

Why the hell did people keep saying that? Schak forced himself to sound calm. "Darren Mitchell was a good friend. This has been hard."

"I'm sorry for your personal loss." Quince clapped his shoulder. "Does Lammers know? Maybe you shouldn't—"

"I'm fine." Schak regretted his tone and wished he could take another warm sip from his flask. "I found this lead, so no, I'm not taking myself off the case."

"Okay." Quince started to say something else, then stopped.

After a long silence, Schak apologized. "I'm just feeling a little sidelined. Jackson has me writing subpoenas for his case, while he interviews witnesses with Evans."

Quince turned to him and grinned. "You're jealous."

"Oh bullshit. That makes me sound gay."

"I didn't mean it like that. It's just obvious that Jackson and Evans have feelings for each other, and he's always favored her."

"Huh." Schak had wondered about it too. "But they both date other people."

"That doesn't change what I'm saying." Quince exited the expressway and headed west on Sixth Avenue toward the Bethel area.

After another silence, Schak tried to explain what he was feeling, something he rarely did. "My body is ready to retire. I've got sore feet and a bad back, and this time of day feels late to be working." He grunted. "But my brain doesn't want to give up the puzzles, and my ego doesn't want to let go of the identity and authority."

"I can understand that," Quince said softly. "Too bad you can't work part time."

"It's not that kind of job."

Quince nodded. "So tell me everything you know about Radovick."

Schak gave him a rundown of the man's file, then added, "I found his current address in the property database. Radovick is listed as a co-owner. I suspect he doesn't want the place directly associated with his name."

"If he's moving drugs or guns, then probably not."

They located the house on a dead-end street where West Eugene butted up against the wetlands. It sat near the back of a large lot that hosted a second smaller home behind the first. At least that was what it looked like from the sidewalk, where they stood staring into the darkness with a light rain falling. Lights were on in both buildings, and the wide gravel driveway hosted a collection of older vehicles, including an oversized van.

"I've got a bad feeling about this," Quince said.

"Yeah. I suspect we'll be outnumbered." Schak pulled out his phone and called Lammers. "We're ready to approach. Where's our backup?"

"They should be there any minute. Or they may already be parked somewhere, waiting. What's the situation?"

"Two houses and four vehicles, including a transport van."

"I'll send another unit." Lammers cleared her throat. "Remember, this is just a lead and can wait until we know more. We could conduct surveillance for a few days first."

The boss was giving him permission to back off—but the delay would also give the perp time to destroy evidence or leave town. Schak offered his usual counterpoint. "Maybe Radovick has gone straight and is running a recovery house, helping ex-cons with their re-entry. So nothing to worry about."

"Fat chance." He heard crinkling sounds in the background, like she was opening a sack of fast food. "Be safe and keep in touch." Lammers clicked off.

A dark-blue SUV rolled up, its engine quiet. Schak jogged over to the driver, a young cop he didn't know. "We're going to the door, and we need you behind us."

"What's the objective?"

"To bring Jorio Radovick in for questioning. Best case scenario, he comes voluntarily."

"And worst-case scenario?" The officer's eyes sparked with anticipation.

"We have to cuff him, and his armed roommates object."

"How many?"

"We don't know. He could be alone and asleep."

"Yeah, right." The officer climbed from the SUV. "I'll get a shotgun."

As they crossed the street to join Quince, another department SUV drove up. The patrol officer stepped out, a man named Chang he'd worked with before.

Schak was starting to feel like he'd made a bad call getting others involved. This could turn out to be a big nothing, with Radovick not even home.

But they had to check him out.

As they huddled in the dark street, Schak gave orders. "Quince and I will approach the door." He gestured at the patrol men. "You two flank us on the sides. Watch for anyone or anything coming from behind the house, especially from the unit in back."

They moved cautiously toward the entrance, each with a hand on their weapons. Music and voices could be heard from within. As they reached the porch, the sounds abruptly shut off. The door opened, and a stocky man bellowed, "This is private property! Get off!"

"Eugene Police!" Schak shouted back. "Step out here with your hands in the air!"

"Do you have a warrant?" The dark-haired guy matched Radovick's mugshot.

"I don't need one. Step outside, or we're coming in."

Radovick reluctantly complied, leaving the door open behind him. "What the hell is this about?"

"Officer Mitchell's murder. We'd like to ask some questions."

"No clue what you're talking about." Behind him, shuffling noises sounded in the house.

How many people were in there? Did they have weapons? "Where were you Thursday morning?"

"I can't remember at the moment."

"Then we'll go into the department and give you time to think about it." Schak stepped toward the man.

"No. I think you have the wrong house. Or the wrong name." Radovick dropped his arms and took a step backward.

That was odd. "Don't move! Put your hands back up!"

A faint, but alarming, sound from the unit in back caught Schak's attention. He glanced left and saw the young officer run around the corner toward the sound. Schak wanted to follow him, but first . . . He looked at the suspect just as Radovick reached around to the back of his jeans.

Gun!

Schak raised his Sig Sauer and fired two shots.

So did Quince.

The sound was deafening. Schak's ears rang as blood sprayed from the holes in Radovick's chest.

Fuck! Schak gulped for air and glanced at Quince. His partner looked stunned but physically fine. Officer Chang ran toward them from his lateral position, his eyes focused on the main house.

Schak glanced back and saw two women inside the door, staring out at Radovick's body on the ground.

"Cuff the suspect and search the house!" Schak shouted orders, then ran left toward the rear of the property. A moment later, he tripped on a cluster of broken ceramic pots, but caught himself, then narrowly missed colliding with an old washing machine.

He cursed under his breath and rounded the corner. Ahead, the young officer had reached the small cottage and was trying to kick in the door. Schak rushed up next to him, wishing he had the SWAT unit's massive doorknocker, but they would have to do it the hard way. "Shoulder slam on three!"

As they smashed into it, the door splintered around the handle and lock. Schak punched through the breakage and unlocked it. They rushed inside, weapons drawn.

The stench was overwhelming, as though the plumbing hadn't worked in years. Boxes, backpacks, and plastic bags were stacked everywhere in the ten-by-ten front room. A young, brown-skinned woman jumped up from the couch. "Policia?"

"Yes! Hands in the air."

She did as instructed, and Schak glanced past the tiny kitchen area at side-by-side interior doors. One stood open, revealing a disgusting bathroom, but the second was closed. Schak ran toward it, as the young officer spoke to the woman in Spanish.

Another locked door. "Damn!" But it was cheap and hollow-core. He kicked it open with one powerful snap—and felt his hamstring tear. Ignoring the pain, he rushed inside. Another young woman stood in the middle of the room, her expression vacillating between terror and joy.

"Police." Schak moved toward her, visually searching her for weapons, but she wore a dirty summer dress and nothing else. "Are you all right?"

The girl burst into tears. "I am now."

Chapter 18

Friday evening

Not bothering to listen to the voice message, Jackson stepped inside and called McCray back. "Hey, what's up?"

"Dagen drove to a house on Olive Street and entered the apartment above the garage. Isn't that the victim's place?"

What the hell? "Yes, and I was just there an hour ago." Jackson looked around for his jacket. "If he tries to leave, stall him. I'll head over."

"He's already on the move. I texted you, but you didn't respond."

"Stay with him and keep me posted. I'll call back when I'm in my car."

The look on Benjie's face when he kissed him goodnight without a story broke Jackson's heart. "We'll have a boys-only day soon, I promise."

"At Putter's? For pizza and arcade games?"

The boy was a skilled negotiator. "Deal." Jackson kissed him goodnight. "Be good for Katie."

Once he was on the street, Jackson called McCray. "Where are you now?"

"Just crossed the Ferry Street Bridge onto Coburg Road."

Good news. "He's probably headed to his mother's house on Roland Way. It's off Oakmont. If he makes that turn, we can hang up."

"Roger that."

A few minutes later, Jackson pulled in behind McCray's old Explorer parked next door to the Hammersmith home. He quickly joined his partner on the sidewalk. In the dark, the house looked smaller and older than it had the day before.

"That's his vehicle," McCray said, pointing at a minivan in the driveway.

"Let's go." As they hurried toward the house, Jackson said, "I'll knock and ask, but we're going in regardless."

"I'm pretty sure I witnessed a crime." McCray spoke and walked softly. "Unless he has a key to the apartment."

"Zena may have given him one, but it doesn't matter. He tampered with a police investigation." Jackson pounded on the door. "Police! Open up!"

Scuffling noises inside the house. Jackson had another sense of *deja vu.* "We're coming in!" He grabbed the knob and turned. Locked. *Damn!* "Police!"

A moment later, the mother opened the door. "What's going on?"

Jackson pushed past her, with McCray on his heels. "Dagen broke into Zena's apartment, and we intend to find out why."

At the end of the hall, Jackson rushed through an open bedroom door. Two overnight bags sat on the bed, half full of clothes, but Dagen wasn't in the room. Jackson spun around and shouted, "Take the front!"

McCray sprinted back up the hall, and Jackson ran for the rear door Dagen had exited the night before. As Jackson stepped outside, he heard a loud engine start. *No!* He started to bolt around the outside of the house, thinking it would be faster, then remembered the fence and troublesome gate. He spun back and charged up the hall and out the door. Dagen's mother stood on the front path, watching her son back into the street. McCray was already inside his Explorer, starting it.

As Jackson ran for his vehicle, McCray gunned his engine and cranked the wheel, slamming to a stop sideways in the road.

Jackson climbed into his sedan and watched behind him as he turned the key. Dagen abruptly stopped, backed up, and jerked the minivan in his direction. Jackson pressed the accelerator and pulled the steering wheel hard to the right. A second later, he slammed to a stop sideways just as McCray had done. Dagen was trapped—unless he decided to go freewheeling over a sidewalk.

Lisha Hammersmith was in the street now, pleading with her son. "Stop and deal with it!"

Dagen finally listened to reason and pulled back into the driveway.

Not willing to take any more chances, Jackson bolted from his car and sprinted toward the minivan. As Dagen climbed out, Jackson spun him and slammed him against the vehicle. He'd had enough of this kid.

Chapter 19

Friday evening

Jackson bought a diet Dr. Pepper from the vending machine and downed half of it. Exhausted from lack of sleep and constant motion, he now had a headache. The caffeine might not fix that, but it would get him through the interrogation.

Evans stepped into the break room, looking fresh and cheeky as always. "Ready?"

"Maybe we should wait until morning. Let the punk sit in that dark hole overnight. He'll be ready to tell us anything we want."

"I respectfully disagree." She gave a tiny wink. "He's still a teenager. Leaving him alone overnight could work against us. He might go comatose and refuse to talk at all, or his mother might be calling a lawyer right now."

Jackson had read Dagen his rights immediately after cuffing him. So far, the young man hadn't asked to make a call. "I don't want to have to book him into jail afterward. I'm hitting the wall."

"I'll do it. I took some Provigil earlier, so I'm good for several more hours."

Jackson envied her prescription for the stay-awake medication. "Thanks. I'll let you."

"Thanks for calling me in. You know how I love interrogations."

Jackson nodded. "You might as well hear it firsthand." He'd dismissed McCray, who was limited by his role as a freelancer. Jackson had also texted Schak, but he hadn't responded.

"Let's go." Evans gestured for him to get moving. "I think we should question him in hour-long sessions, then let him sit long enough to think we had time to gather more evidence, then go at him again."

"I'll need another Dr. Pepper."

As he followed Evans downstairs, he wondered when and if he would tell her about Kera moving out. It could wait until they'd wrapped up the main push of their investigation.

Dagen had his head down on the table, his cuffed wrists out in front. He wore the same gray sweatshirt he'd had on yesterday. Maybe Dagen had been at Skinner's Butte Thursday morning when the body was found. So far, patrol officers hadn't picked up anyone matching the description of the boys they'd seen, but Mitchell's shooting had been a priority.

Dagen looked up. "This is all a misunderstanding."

"That's what all killers say." Evans smiled and took a seat near the wall.

Jackson eased into the other chair and downed another gulp of soda.

"Can I have one of those? I'm really thirsty."

Jackson pointed at the plastic cup of water he'd left with him. "Drink that."

"I can't drink plain water. It makes me gag."

Evans made a noise in her throat. "I'm sure they'll treat your kidney stones in prison." She'd apparently decided to play bad cop this time.

Probably her prescription. Jackson decided to take the lead and let her inject daggers of fear every once in a while. "Let's start at the beginning." Jackson resigned himself to being there all night. "How did you meet Zena?"

"At Starbucks. I go there every day, and she was really friendly with me."

On impulse, Jackson shot back, "Where do you get the money to spend five dollars a day on lattes?"

"Well, not every single day. But I work as a dog walker sometimes."

Huh. "When did you and Zena start dating?" Teenagers didn't use that term anymore, but Jackson didn't care.

"Uh, in August sometime."

"Did she have phone service?"

Dagen squinted in confusion. "Of course. Everybody does."

So they'd started seeing each other after August 3. Jackson made notes. Timelines could be critical, especially once they had phone records. "When did you find out Zena was pregnant?"

Rapid blinking and a dry swallow. "She was pregnant? I didn't know."

Evans shook her head. "You're not very convincing."

"Why would I lie about it?" Dagen tried to sound sincere.

"For the same reason you lied about when you left your friend's house the night Zena died." Jackson raised his voice. "You're covering your tracks. That's why you took Zena's journal."

"What?" He made a face suggesting they were crazy. "I don't know what you're talking about."

More bullshit. "The notebook Zena kept is missing from her apartment. You were the only other person who had access, and you went in there after she was killed."

"I never saw it." His delivery was deadpan, as though he was controlling his emotions. "Maybe she kept it hidden."

Evans shook her head. "You're not a good liar."

Jackson would circle back to the journal. "Tell us about the fight between you and Zena. Was that about her pregnancy?"

"What fight?" Sweat shimmered on his pale forehead.

"Ruby, the landlady, heard it all. So we already know, and we want to see if you can tell the truth about anything." Lying to suspects was a standard interrogation tactic, but Jackson had mixed feelings about it. Unless a suspect lied to him, then all bets were off.

Pale and scared, Dagen finally sipped some water. "Yeah, Zena told me she was pregnant and that I could walk away." He lifted his cuffed hands and wiped his forehead. "I suggested she get an abortion, but she refused. She didn't want to give it up for adoption either. She said she couldn't stand knowing she had a kid out there and not be able to make sure he had a good life." For the first time, Dagen's voice cracked with real emotion. "Zena was such a good person, but I wasn't ready to be a father."

Was this his breaking point? First sympathize. "I understand that feeling." Then drill down. "So you needed to control the situation, and killing Zena and the baby was the only way to protect yourself."

"No! I'm just explaining why I wanted her to have an abortion. I'm not a monster."

Jackson would keep circling back until Dagen got closer and closer to the truth, then finally confessed. "Why did you break into her apartment this evening?"

"I didn't break in. I used the spare key Zena had hidden."

"The question was *why*."

Dagen's shoulders slumped. "I was looking for her journal."

"So you do know about it." *Had he told the truth about anything?*

"She mentioned it once."

"We know you already took it," Evans pressed. "Right after you caused Zena's death. You left her dying on Skinner's Butte, then went straight to her apartment to destroy evidence of your involvement."

"No! I didn't hurt her, and I don't have the journal!" Feisty, but near tears.

If that was true, then someone else had taken it, or Zena had given it to someone for safekeeping. Jackson leaned forward. You admitted you were looking for it. What's your interest in the journal?"

Dagen sighed. "I wanted to see if she mentioned the baby's father. I started to think it wasn't mine."

"Why?"

He blushed as he looked away. "We only had sex a few times, and I thought girls didn't know until after six weeks."

"Did she take a home pregnancy test?" Evans asked.

"I think so."

"Did you see it?" Evans pressed. "Or did she refuse to show you the results?"

Dagen squirmed in his chair.

"You said earlier that you thought Zena was cheating on you," Evans reminded him. "Maybe you thought it was the other guy's kid. I can see why you would want her and the baby dead."

Dagen shook his head. "Stop saying that. I just wanted the truth." A pause. "And for her not to be pregnant." He blinked back tears. "She was my first girlfriend, and I really liked her."

This was getting nowhere. "Do you know anyone who didn't like her?" Jackson asked on a whim. "Maybe someone who hated Zena enough to want her dead?"

A long silence, then another sigh. "My mother."

Chapter 20

Friday evening

Schak stared at the captive girl, who'd been held in a locked room. What now? She might need medical care, and all of the women needed social services to find them a place to stay and help them get home. That wasn't his department.

"Clear the place, then call social services," he directed the young officer. Schak wanted to search the main house for more captives.

As he opened the front door, a gunshot boomed. Heart racing, he turned to the others and shouted, "Stay in here!"

Schak rushed outside, his weapon still in hand, and ran toward the main house. He rounded the corner and saw Quince and Chang on the ground. Chang was belly crawling toward the garage for cover, while Quince fired at a front window from his ground-level position.

More shots rang out from the house.

Shit! For a moment, Schak felt paralyzed. Shooters on the inside always had the advantage, with better sightlines and better cover. They needed more help. He stepped back around the corner out of sight, flattened himself against the wall, and pressed 911.

"What's your emergency?"

"Shots fired. Officers down. Send the SWAT unit!" Schak rattled off the address and ended the call.

He stuck his head around the corner and looked for Quince. His partner had crawled behind the junker washing machine. But where were the two women he'd seen in the doorway earlier?

Schak pounded the exterior wall and yelled at the top of his voice. "Put down your weapons! You can't escape!"

A bullet ripped through the siding next to him. Schak spotted a wheelbarrow in the yard, sprinted the twenty feet, and squatted behind it.

He edged out to the side and saw Quince stand and fire. A moment later, his partner emptied his clip. Now Quince was just a target. Detectives didn't carry extra munitions. They rarely had to use their weapons.

Schak bolted to his feet, fired three rounds, and dropped back down. Shots echoed from the garage as Chang took up the gunfight.

For a moment, the night was quiet, then sirens sounded on a nearby street, breaking the silence. More patrol units! The SWAT crew would take longer, but they were assembling. Schak's pulse slowed a little, but his chest felt so tight, he worried he might have another heart attack.

Chapter 21

Around the same time

Evans led Dagen upstairs, preparing to take him to the county jail, where she would list obstruction of justice and lying to a police officer as charges. Jackson followed her up, most likely heading home. As they entered the lobby, her phone rang. She slipped it out of her pocket and checked the screen: *Sergeant Bruckner.*

A SWAT callout! Adrenaline started to flow, and her pulse quickened. "Jackson! Take the suspect. It's Bruckner." She let go of Dagen and answered the call. "What have we got?"

"A shooter inside a house, refusing to surrender. Another suspect shot and possibly dead outside."

"Any hostages?"

"Two women. Two others already rescued." A pause. "Your buddy Schakowski called it in."

Schak? What the hell? "He's working Mitchell's homicide."

"Sounds like we've got cop killers. Where are you now? I'll text you the address."

"At the department. I'll see you in five." Evans clicked off and looked at Jackson. "A shooter and hostages, with Schak somehow involved. I have to go but I'll update you if I can." She ran for the wide front door.

"Be safe!" Jackson called after her.

At the police complex on Second and Chambers, Evans pulled gear from her locker and quickly changed into tactical fatigues, including boots and a Kevlar vest. After grabbing her assault rifle, she slammed the locker shut and ran out to the side parking lot. A deep-blue armored truck—nicknamed Barney and loaded with weapons, flashbangs, and teargas— sat waiting with the back doors open as team members climbed inside. Sergeant Bruckner stood nearby, his massive presence intimidating.

But Evans decided to buck the protocol. "Sir, I'm taking my own car. The scene is only five minutes from my house, and I might need to regroup with the taskforce rather than come back here."

Bruckner nodded. "See you out there."

Evans ran to her sedan and raced toward the scene, trying to connect the pieces. Schak had apparently identified a suspect in the cop shootings, then gone out to question him. But why were there female hostages?

Six minutes later, she turned down a side street and swerved around the portable barrier. A uniformed officer stood next to three citizens on the corner, keeping them from getting any closer to the scene. *Residents who'd been evacuated.* She noticed the street was mostly open terrain, with only five houses, a few trees, and no fences—offering almost no cover to the SWAT members. The single streetlight though gave off so little light, they would at least have the cover of darkness.

A row of patrol units sat along the left side, and Evans parked behind them. At the front of the line, she spotted Schak's sedan, then felt a pang of jealously that he'd found a lead and a suspect in such an important case. But she was also grateful. No officer was safe until the perps were apprehended. Or dead.

Squinting in the dark, Evans jogged along the line of police SUVs to the cluster of officers gathered behind the first one. As she approached, she spotted Schak and Quince. "Hey," she called softly, "Evans here."

The men all turned, and Schak asked, "Where's the truck and team?"

"En route. I drove my car."

"Too bad you're not a sniper," Schak said. "I'm pretty sure there's only one shooter in there."

"What's the status? Any shots fired recently?"

"Quiet for the last ten minutes."

"Where are the hostages being held?" Evans asked.

"We don't know." Quince shook his head. "The women were standing near the doorway when Radovick came outside. After he pulled a weapon, we shot him, then the door slammed. We haven't seen or heard from them since."

"Are we sure they're hostages and not conspirators?"

"Almost certain." Schak sounded like he was in pain. "One of the women we rescued was locked in a room. I think they're being trafficked."

"Where are those two?"

Schak pointed at a small house near the back of the property. "An officer is with them, but you might go see if they need anything."

Evans shook the head. "I'm here as a SWAT member, trained in special entry. I'll wait for Bruckner to give my orders."

A big engine rumbled, and she turned to see the armored truck rolling toward them. It drove past and parked two houses away. A dozen men in tactical gear filed out, and

Bruckner climbed out of the front. He pointed at neighboring roofs and a single tall pine, and the snipers moved quickly to get into place.

She jogged over and stood with her team, waiting for her assignment.

"The hasty team will take secondary positions until we're ready to move in," Bruckner said. "We just don't have enough cover to get close. So we'll give the hostage negotiator as much time as he needs." Bruckner nodded at Evans. "Position yourself behind that stump in the next yard over."

Pleased she'd been singled out, Evans hustled over to the barricade. As the smallest and most agile person on the team, she was best equipped to conduct recon or quietly enter the house from the back, if necessary. She squatted down behind the three-foot stump and prepared to wait. It could be a long night.

Chapter 22

Saturday, Oct. 3, 6:53 a.m.

Jackson woke, instantly aware that something was different, that he was alone. The moment didn't last long. Benjie padded into the room and stood by the bed, his face next to Jackson's. "Morning, Daddy."

"Good morning, son. Did you sleep well?"

"I think so." The boy squinted his eyes. "Where's Kera? And Micah?"

Jackson sat up. He hadn't had time to plan what he would say. "They're staying with Micah's grandpa for a while." *Mostly true.* "He's lonely and misses Micah."

"I miss Micah." Benjie giggled. "Except when he cries at night and takes my toys."

Jackson pulled on pants and checked the clock. *Oh hell.* The alarm hadn't gone off.

"Daddy?"

Jackson cringed. He knew that worried tone. "Yes?"

"Kera's not coming back, is she?" Benjie's sweet little eyes watered as he climbed on the bed.

Oh no. The boy never cried. Why was he so perceptive? "I don't know for sure." Jackson picked him up and hugged him tight. "But you'll see her again sometimes. We'll be okay."

After breakfast, Jackson checked his phone again. No messages from Schak or Evans. Not knowing anything was driving him crazy. He was especially worried about Evans. The last time she'd gone out on a SWAT call, she'd tried to rescue a child and ended up a hostage. He couldn't bear the thought of losing her, now that he was moments away from telling her how he felt.

He wanted to check in with Lammers, but resisted. She was probably deep in paperwork, phone calls, and bureaucracy handling the officer shootings and the hostage situation. The press was probably hounding her too. Sophie Speranza, a reporter for the *Willamette News*, had left him several voice messages, but Jackson wouldn't return her calls until he actually knew something. The best thing he could do was focus on work.

He sat down at his desk in the living room while Benjie played with Legos on the floor next to him. His first task was to read the background summary Evans had done for Lisha Hammersmith. Jackson hadn't considered her a viable murder suspect—until Dagen's admission the night before—but he would be open minded now.

Lisha had lived in Eugene for twenty-six years without ever being arrested. She'd been Lisa Mercer on her marriage application to Mark Hammersmith, then apparently had added the *H* to her first name when she'd legally made the change to her husband's surname. She'd given birth to Dagen three years later, then divorced six years after that but kept her husband's name. Lisha had been employed by the city of Eugene as a librarian for ten years before filing for disability.

Jackson sat back, unsurprised. Nothing in her file indicated she was capable of murder. Yet Dagen had claimed his mother once said she would rather Zena die than ruin his life. Lisha had also refused to let them search Dagen's room for the journal when they'd picked him up, so it was time to ask a few more questions.

As he stood to leave, his phone beeped with a text. Konrad, the pathologist, had sent a message: *Prelim toxicology report for Zena Summers indicates a lethal level of fentanyl in her blood, but none in her hair or nails, so she wasn't a long-term user. Cause of death: opioid overdose.*

Jackson sighed. Fentanyl, one of the most powerful narcotics available, was now a factor in forty percent of drug overdoses. It was typically laced into other substances, such as heroin or counterfeit Oxycontin pills. The users often didn't know. As a medication, doctors only prescribed it to people dying of cancer or patients with chronic pain who'd become tolerant of other meds. He thought about the tiny pouch he'd found in Zena's freezer.

Had she killed herself or had someone injected her?

For the third time in three days, Jackson knocked on the Hammersmiths' door. Lisha took her time opening it, then snapped, "Where is Dagen?" Her eyes were clearer than the previous times he'd been there, and her tone sharper, but she was dressed in a housecoat.

"In jail, charged with obstructing justice." Jackson started to threaten her with the same charge, but she cut him off.

"That's crazy. When is his arraignment? He needs to be released into my custody." The woman leaned on a cane—the first time he'd seen her with it—her voice seeming bigger than her body.

Jackson feared she wouldn't cooperate, and he would have to take her in. "You'll have to call the jail about that. Right now, you need to answer more questions. May I come in?" He hoped to keep Dagen locked up until they could access his phone records.

"There's nothing else to say."

Time to be aggressive. "Dagen had a lot to say about your feelings for Zena. In fact, he suggested you might have killed her. We can either talk about it here or at the department." Dagen had only hinted at the possibility, but he'd definitely thrown his mother under the bus.

Lisha gasped, then pressed a hand to her chest. "I don't believe you. Nor do I feel well enough to deal with this." She tried to close the door.

Jackson blocked it with his foot. "This isn't optional. I will cuff you and take you in for questioning. You'll find our interrogation room to be both unpleasant and uncomfortable." She might end up there anyway, but he wanted his report to reflect that he'd given her options.

"You wouldn't dare." She wiggled her cane at him. "I would sue the department, and they would settle to avoid public embarrassment."

Anger burned in his chest. "Why are you so afraid to answer questions?" He wasn't afraid to take her into custody. All he needed was a medical transport or a judge's order for a house arrest ankle bracelet, but he desperately didn't want it to go that way.

Some of the defiance went out of her eyes. "I'm just tired of being harassed."

"A young, pregnant girl is dead, likely murdered." Jackson pushed the door open with his foot. "And I intend to find out who is responsible."

Lisha glared for a long moment, then stepped back. "I'll give you ten minutes. After that I need to lie down."

Jackson entered the home and moved toward the kitchen table. "Let's sit here." When she joined him, he shifted tactics, hoping to move beyond the antagonism. "What condition do you have?"

"Depends on who you ask." Lisha let out a long sigh. "The medical consensus seems to be that I have two autoimmune diseases, Lupus and Myositis, and they both cause chronic pain."

A reason to take powerful medication. "I'm sorry to hear that. It must make life difficult."

"It does." Her expression softened. "But the coronavirus vaccine gave me some relief for about a year. Some researchers now think that viruses could be the cause of most autoimmune diseases, so I'm optimistic they'll soon find a cure for all of us."

Jackson was intrigued, but he couldn't let himself get sidetracked. "Do you have a prescription for your pain?"

A wary look. "Yes. Why?"

"What do you take?"

"Duragesic."

"Is that a fentanyl patch?"

"Yes."

Could she have killed Zena with a patch? Told her it was something else? "How quickly does it work?"

"It's not like taking a pill. You have to build up enough in your skin before it will pass into your body, then . . . " Lisha stopped and shook her head. "Why are you asking me this?"

Jackson decided to let that subject go for the moment. He needed Lisha to talk about her animosity toward the victim. "Why did you hate Zena?"

Lisha glanced over at the kitchen. "I didn't hate her."

"Dagen says you did. He claims you wanted her dead rather than part of his life. Why?"

The mother pushed her hands through her thinning hair, then clamped her teeth, resigned. "Zena derailed Dagen. Totally and completely. He had finally enrolled in community college with an actual goal of getting some kind of tech degree. Then she came along, and he lost his focus." Lisha let out a harsh laugh. "Lost his freakin' mind. I'm sure it was about having sex for the first time, then becoming obsessed with getting more."

"That sounds temporary and pretty normal. Why so much anger at Zena?"

"You don't know Dagen. He's been glued to a video game for the last decade. I tried everything to get him to do something with his life, but he wouldn't listen." Lisha drank from a cup that was already on the table. "So I tried a new tactic. A compromise. I convinced him to study coding so he could learn to write his own games. He was actually kind of excited about starting the program. Then he met Zena, and she turned him off the idea." Lisha's face tightened with bitterness.

Parents had killed other people's teenagers for less. Jackson had to remind himself that Lisha's frailty could be somewhat of an act. Her new cane, for example, could be a prop. She was certainly capable of the emotions associated with a murderous rage.

"Where were you Wednesday night between ten and two the next morning?" He'd asked the first time, but it was always interesting to see if the answer changed.

"Right here. As I told you."

"Can you corroborate that?"

The woman scowled. "How? I didn't have any company."

"Dagen says you went out for a while and were still gone when he left. Where did you go?"

She looked stunned and angry. "I went to the store because I needed popcorn. It's my late night comfort food."

"What time?"

"I'm not sure. But I think it was around eight-thirty."

"Which store?"

"The Safeway on Eighteenth."

"Where Zena worked."

Lisha rolled her eyes. "So? It's the closest one."

"Why did you lie about it?"

"I didn't lie. It just didn't seem important."

"In a murder investigation?"

Silence.

"What time did you get home?" So far, her and Dagen's timelines weren't matching up.

"I don't know. I was only gone for about twenty-five minutes."

Jackson would come back to that too and check with her neighbors. At the moment, she was rattled, and he needed to press the advantage. "Why did you send Dagen to Zena's apartment to search for her journal? What's in there that you want to hide?"

"That's ridiculous." Lisha pushed up from the table, unsteady. "I need to lie down." She started to walk away, then turned back. "You're not a nice man."

He'd been called worse—and he wasn't done. "Are you going to let Dagen go to prison for a murder you committed?" Jackson stood too.

"I told you, she probably killed herself!"

Interesting that she kept saying that. "You act like you know how she died."

"I don't know anything, except that I'm in pain." Lisha limped toward the hall.

Jackson followed her. "I need to search for Zena's journal. You don't mind, do you?" Likely a waste of time. Either she or Dagen had probably destroyed it by now.

"I resent it, but I won't stop you." She glanced over her shoulder. "And I'm too tired to follow you around."

"I also need to see your fentanyl patches and whatever other medication you have."

Lisha turned and stared. "Seriously?"

"You seem to know that Zena died of an overdose, which I've never mentioned. And yes, it was fentanyl. You also lied about your activities the night of the murder. So I have enough circumstantial evidence to get a subpoena for your entire home and your medical records."

Fear flashed in her eyes for the first time. "I'm calling a lawyer."

Chapter 23

Saturday, 9:05 a.m.

Dallas returned from a five-mile run along the river, then showered and dressed in jeans and a T-shirt. The outfit would be okay for the moment, but she needed to hit St. Vincent's to pick up a duffle-bag full of other clothes. What else would she need from her own luggage? Makeup and shampoo, plus a few weapons.

She removed her palm-sized handgun from the locked case she'd traveled with and tucked it into the secret compartment in the bottom of her purse. Being a federal agent had its perks. Her switchblade could slide into a pocket of whatever she wore. Where to hide her phone was a more worrisome question. Because it had a camera, her burner was larger than most of the cheap versions. Her concern was that someone from the cult might search her body and personal items before allowing her into the compound. Paranoid types were like that. In the prepper community she'd infiltrated, they'd monitored digital communications, so she'd been completely cut off from her handler.

Dallas opened the panel that held the gun, a Saturday Night Special, and wedged the phone in next to it. The fit was tight, but it worked. Goddard might not care that she had it, but instinct told her the anti-technology group had rules about such things. If they confiscated it and searched her contacts, she would be burned.

The shopping spree at the second-hand store took longer than she would have liked, but as she'd chosen items, she'd made up little stories about them. The tarnished mirror with the fake-jewel frame, for example, had been *a present from her father on her tenth birthday. He'd died of cancer soon after.* Background details were essential to credibility.

Trust took time though, and she wanted to work quickly, so her next stop was at SweetTree Farms. Inside the fragrant store, she bought a potent cannabis tincture that she could use to sedate her target and picked up some sativa buds too. Augie obviously drank alcohol, so he might also voluntarily indulge in smokable weed. When people were high, they tended to spill their secrets. She had a tolerance for almost everything, but she'd recently discovered that marijuana intensified her sexual desire and pleasure, so she would have to be careful. As a first line of pliability, alcohol was better, so she stopped at a liquor store and bought three bottles of vodka. It annoyed her to make a separate trip to a grocery store for food, but Oregon only sold hard alcohol in state-run businesses. Yet you could buy pot on every other corner.

In the car, she munched on an apple as she drove to Blair Alley and parked behind the tavern again. The venue was quieter this time, with no DJ and only a few pinball machines clanking. Dallas was tempted to order a beer, but resisted. She might have to drink a boatload of vodka over the next few days to accomplish her goals. At the bar counter, she asked for a lemonade, then started a conversation with the thirty-something man on the next barstool. *Thirty-something* used to refer to other people's ages, but she'd recently hit that milestone. Dallas tried not to let it bother her. She could still pass for a college student. But for how long? And would the best undercover gigs start going to younger agents?

When she caught sight of Augie at the door, she touched barstool-guy's arm and laughed softly. A little FOMO would be good for her target and inspire him to act quickly. Augie responded as predicted and rushed over, then hugged her hard and spun her away from the other man.

"I'm so happy to see you." He beamed with pleasure. "After you walked out of here last night, I worried that I'd never see you again."

Dallas laughed. "I'm too broke to go anywhere." She paused. "And I like you."

"Best thing I've heard all day."

The bartender walked up, so Augie ordered a beer and a sandwich, then turned to Dallas. "Do you want anything? I'm buying."

"I'm fine, but thanks." It was best to seem reluctant to take any help, regardless of her financial circumstances.

He ordered her a honey beer anyway. "I feel like celebrating."

"What's the occasion?"

"Meeting you!" He smiled and stroked her arm. "I made an important decision too. Kind of a fresh start."

"Sounds intriguing. Want to tell me about it?"

"It's complicated. But I plan to make a break from my family when I've saved up enough money."

Did he mean the cult? If he was poised to leave, that could be both good and bad. "Do you still live with your parents?" So many young people did that it wasn't a shameful status anymore.

"Sort of." Augie sipped his beer and watched as the bartender set down his food. He handed over cash, then asked Dallas, "How long have you been on your own?"

"A few years. I'm twenty-two, if that's what you're asking."

He smiled. "You're different than other girls. More mature. I worried that you might be older."

Dallas laughed. "No one has ever called me *mature* before." She touched her face. "Living in my car must have aged me."

"No! I didn't mean that. You're beautiful."

"Thanks." But the comment bothered her. Maybe it was time to start using retinol and other age-defying skin products.

They spent the afternoon walking around the Whitaker neighborhood and sampling beer from the various breweries. If Augie had been even slightly intellectual, Dallas would have enjoyed herself. But he mostly talked about his job at the garden store and how demanding the customers were. Dallas brought up the subject of technology and social media a few times, but Augie seemed indifferent, saying only, "It's a tool that can be helpful or destructive, depending on how you use it." That was the most interesting thing that came out of his mouth.

Until he kissed her and tried to press his tongue. Dallas gave him some leeway, then pulled back. "Let's get to know each other a little better."

"I'm good with that." Augie grabbed her hand, and they walked back toward the pinball tavern.

In the parking lot, Dallas stopped at her beat-up Toyota filled with crap. "I really enjoyed this afternoon."

After glancing inside her car, Augie stared into her eyes for a long moment. "This date doesn't have to end."

"What do you mean?"

"You can come with me to the place where I live. It's secluded and unusual, but the people are friendly." He swallowed, then added. "You'll be welcome."

"You mean like a commune?"

"Sort of." Augie took a long breath. "I grew up there, and I had a simple but mostly happy life. But now that I'm spending more time outside the compound, I'm reassessing a few things."

Dallas smiled. "That's what we're supposed to do at this age." She let her smile fade. "I'm trying to figure out how to continue my massage business without a phone or a laptop. I haven't missed the drama and distraction of being online, but I do need a way for people to contact me."

"Yeah. It's a dilemma, but maybe we can figure out things together."

Dallas pressed her lips together, as if trying to make up her mind.

"It's better than sleeping in your car. I have a little place with a bathroom and a kitchen. Luxurious!" Augie laughed.

Dallas gave him her hundred-watt smile. "It can't hurt to check it out."

Chapter 24

Saturday, 10:15 a.m.

Evans' legs cramped, so she stretched out on the ground again, belly and elbows down. She'd been rotating between squat and soldier mode for nearly ten hours and had endured a long episode of light rain just before dawn. But the pain kept her awake. Bruckner had pulled her out of position once so she could relieve herself and get her circulation flowing, but she was desperate to move again. That moment was coming. The hostage negotiator had finally given up after the suspect, identified as Manny Kronin, had insisted that he be allowed to flee and take one of the hostages with him.

Evans leaned out to check the house again and spotted someone in a window on her side. She pressed the call button on her shoulder radio. "Evans here. I see movement on this end. I think the hostages may have been separated."

"Can you get closer to confirm?"

"Roger that." Evans clicked off, pushed her assault rifle around to her back, and started belly crawling. The ground under the dried-out lawn was packed hard and littered with painful clumps of dirt and rock, but at least she was on the move.

From the street, Bruckner used his bullhorn to shout at the hostage taker. "Put your weapon down and come out with your hands up!" He was engaging the perp while she crossed the yard to the old washing machine near the front of the house.

The woman she'd spotted was now visible in the window not far from her. *A bathroom,* she suspected. Not waiting to ask permission, Evans crawled from behind the appliance and quickly scooted to the house, catching sight of a dead body near the front door. It had to be one of the shooters.

With her back against the wall, she pushed up until her head was near the bottom corner of the window. Using her flashlight, she reached up and over to tap once on the glass.

Startled movement inside, followed by the quiet sound of metal slowly sliding against metal. The old house had never been updated with vinyl frames. A voice whispered, "Policia?"

"Yes. Can you climb out?" Evans spoke as softly as possible. "I can help."

Another strange metal noise. Evans glanced over and saw the screen gently bulge out. "Push!" A more urgent whisper.

In the distance, Bruckner continued to shout at the perp through his bullhorn. Evans knew that a team member was watching her closely through night-vision binoculars. She pulled her utility knife, slipped the blade under the screen, and popped the mesh frame out of place. The screen dropped down, but she caught it just before it banged into the house.

A young woman leaned out of the window, her expression terrified.

Evans scooted under the sill, bent over, and reached up to tap her own backside, indicating her body should be used as a step down. "Now!" she commanded in a harsh whisper.

The woman whimpered, then a moment later, a foot pressed into Evans' back. She braced for more weight, but the hostage quickly hopped the rest of the way down, stumbling as she landed. "On your belly!" Evans pushed on the woman's shoulder until she complied.

As they crawled to safety, Bruckner kept shouting.

Behind the neighbor's fence, Evans stood, and the woman followed suit. Evans grabbed her hand and ran for the big truck.

After they learned her name and assessed that she was unhurt, Bruckner handed the rescued hostage a paper tablet. Someone had drawn a crude layout of the house. "Show us where the other woman is," Bruckner said.

Mariana pointed to a bedroom in the back right corner, then looked up. "After Jorio dead, Manny stayed in front room."

With that information, Bruckner decided to send the team inside. "Get the doorknocker!"

As members rushed inside the truck to retrieve it, Mariana broke into sobs. "I want to escape, but they watch us all the time. Five days!"

The men came back out, carrying a heavy four-foot metal cylinder. They would use it to push the door off its hinges and take out anything the perp had stacked against it.

"Hasty team leads with flash bangs," Bruckner commanded. "Stay clear of the perp. Snipers are alert for the signal."

He gestured at her. "Evans, stand down."

"But I—"

"Did a great job," Bruckner interjected. "Still, it was physically taxing, and I have ten other guys who've been standing around all night." He checked to see that everyone was in place and ready. "Go!"

As her team charged into the house, Evans tensed. This was the most dangerous moment.

Less than a minute later, gunshots rang out, then silence.

Evans held her breath.

She heard muffled shouting and boots clumping inside the house, then a radio call to Bruckner. "Perp down and needs an ambulance. Second hostage safe."

Evans breathed a sigh of relief.

Bruckner grinned. "Well done."

"Thank you, sir."

Chapter 25

Around the same time

Lisha Hammersmith put her phone back in her pocket and glared at Jackson. "Just because I can't reach a lawyer on Saturday doesn't mean you can pressure me. I'm quite sure they would advise me not to answer any more questions."

"I'll try not to ask any," Jackson offered. "But I need to find Zena's journal. If Dagen took it—and he admitted he went there to search for it—we both need to know why it's so important. If you're innocent, her notes could actually clear you."

The distressed mother put her head in her hands and stayed silent.

Jackson waited her out.

Finally, she looked up. "All right. Search for the journal in Dagen's room. But he didn't kill her, and neither did I. You should check out her controlling family."

Jackson intended to. "What do you know about them?"

"Nothing, except that Dagen told me she was afraid."

"I'll get started." Jackson headed for the hall.

Lisha followed him. "I'm recording you with my phone to make sure you don't plant evidence."

The new nature of police work. Jackson resented all the bad cops who'd tarnished the respect and trust law enforcement used to have.

Dagen's partially packed overnight bag still sat on the bed. Jackson put on latex gloves, mostly for the sake of Lisha's camera, and pulled out the clothes. At the bottom, he found tennis shoes and in the outside pocket a toothbrush and a razor. No journal. He told himself to let it go. Lisha could have burned it in the fireplace shortly after they took her son into custody. Or Dagen could have thrown it away before he got home, even with McCray watching . . . at a distance, in the dark.

The minivan! Dagen might have left it in his vehicle, thinking he was getting right back into it with his travel bag. Jackson made a mental note to search it before he left. But first, a quick sweep of the room. Nothing was hidden under the clusters of dirty clothes on the floor, and the closet was a bust too, filled only with old toys and other sentimental junk. In the top dresser drawer, he found condoms, a small vibrator ring, and pocketknife hidden under the socks. Besides electronics—TV, laptop, and gaming equipment—the room was relatively sparse. Jackson turned to Lisha. "Do you mind if I access his laptop and check his emails?" *Wishful thinking.*

Lisha shook her head. "Absolutely not."

"Then I'll get a subpoena." Jackson gave her a friendly smile. "Does Dagen have another place in the home where he stores his things? A closet or shelf?"

"No." Lisha stopped the recording, her hands shaking. "I need pain medication," she mumbled, as though to herself.

Jackson followed her out of the room. "I'd like to see where you keep it."

"You're a pain in the ass."

But she hadn't said no, so he followed her into the master bedroom, where she reached for a metal case on a nightstand. Lisha pulled a key from her housecoat and unlocked the case. Jackson wanted to step forward and look inside, but he didn't press his luck.

The woman pulled out a bandaid-sized box, then removed a small, sealed pouch.

It looked similar to the item he'd found in Zena's freezer.

Lisha opened the pouch and extracted a clear one-inch-square patch, then turned to him. "You want to watch me apply it too?" Heavy sarcasm in her tone.

Undaunted, Jackson smiled again. "Yes. I'm intrigued."

"You're a weird pain in the ass." She pushed open her housecoat, lifted her shirt with one hand, and pressed the patch to her abdomen with the other. "Happy now?"

A vivid scenario played out in Jackson's mind—Dagen applying several patches to Zena's belly after she fell asleep, dragging her out to his minivan, then dumping her at the top of Skinner's Butte. Would the adhesive have shown up on Zena's skin? He'd have to ask the pathologist.

Lisha picked up the outer box, scowled, then dumped the contents into her hand.

Jackson counted three pouches.

"Huh. I thought I had more."

Some were missing? "Does Dagen have a key to your medication case?"

More scowling. "Of course not."

"Is this your only supply? Do you keep more pain medication anywhere?"

She let out a long sigh. "I have an injectable for emergency use."

"Also fentanyl? Where do you keep it?"

Lisha pointed at the metal case, sighed again, then picked it up and held it out.

In the corner, sat a tiny bottle of clear liquid with a stopper-style cap and next to it a syringe.

The pathologist had mentioned an injection site on Zena's upper arm. Lisha or Dagen could have lied to Zena about the drug, injected her with an overdose, then dropped her off at the butte to stumble around until she died. Could the lab compare this medication to what was in Zena's bloodstream? Yes, but he would have to take the bottle as evidence. "Can I—"

"No."

"I'll be back with a subpoena."

Out on the sidewalk, Jackson considered his next move. Lisha seemed like a viable suspect despite her frailty. She had motive, means, and opportunity. Still, killing a young girl so her son would go back to college? *Bizarre.* But Lisha did seem overly protective of Dagen. Maybe there was more to the story. *Such as the pregnancy,* Jackson reminded himself. Lisha may have dreaded the idea of her son—and herself—being saddled with a child who probably wasn't theirs.

According to the timeline, Zena had been pregnant when she left the cult. Determining the father might prove to be impossible, even with Dallas' inside help.

Since he was already there, Jackson decided to chat with the neighbors and see if he could verify Lisha's movements the night of the murder. He still didn't know when she'd left the house or returned. He also hoped to hear some useful gossip about the mother and son. Maybe they had gone out together that evening with the intent of eliminating a child neither of them wanted.

The old man who lived next door on the right was so hard of hearing Jackson abandoned the interview after a few minutes. The guy claimed to be asleep by eight every evening, and Jackson had no reason to doubt him. He walked to the other side of the Hammersmiths' and knocked on a newish, faux-Victorian house.

A woman opened the door almost immediately. Tall, with dyed-brown hair, she looked like a well-preserved fifty. "What's going on?" she asked. "Why are you canvassing the neighborhood?"

She'd been watching him out the window. A good sign for his purposes. "Detective Jackson, Eugene Police. I need to ask a few questions."

The neighbor nodded. "Can we sit out here on the porch? I've been waiting for the sun to break through, and now that it has, I want to enjoy it. These nice days are numbered."

"Sure. What's your name?"

"Peggy Davis. Nice to meet you. Would you like some coffee or tea?"

Coffee sounded great, but he never drank from open containers offered by strangers. "I'm fine, but thank you."

"I'll grab my tea and be right back. Have a seat." She left the door open and returned a moment later.

They sat in canvas deck chairs with a glass table between them, and Jackson enjoyed a moment of quiet pleasure as gentle fall sunshine warmed his face.

But he had work to do. "How well do you know your neighbors Lisha and her son Dagen?"

"Not well. I've tried to be friendly with Lisha, but she's not receptive." Peggy sipped her tea. "She mentioned she has Lupus, and I know that can be painful."

"Is she home most of the time?"

"Yes. But I think she attends church on Sundays." A pause. "She works outside in her yard all summer, so I don't think she's as disabled as she claims." Peggy glanced over. "I hope that didn't sound petty."

"I appreciate the information." *What did it mean though? Was Lisha faking her pain to collect disability or was she just addicted to a powerful opioid?* "Do the mother and son get along?"

"As far as I know. I've heard Lisha yell at him to get out of bed in the morning, but I had a kid like that too." Peggy smiled warmly.

Jackson decided she was rather pretty and likable. "Did you ever meet his new girlfriend, Zena?"

"I saw her once, but we didn't meet. Dagen would chat with me sometimes when he was younger, but not lately."

"Were you home on Wednesday night?"

"Yes. I'm here a lot too. I'm a novelist."

Jackson knew he should say something nice, but he was too focused on pinning down Lisha's movements the night of Zena's death. So he just smiled. "Did you see Lisha leave her house that evening?"

"Wednesday. Uh, that's recycling day." The neighbor set down her cup. "Oh yeah. When I went out kind of late to bring in my containers, I saw her backing out in the Honda. I think it was around nine-thirty or so."

That didn't line up with what Lisha had claimed. "Did you see her come home?"

She shook her head. "Sorry. I did some more writing, then watched a movie."

"Did you see Dagen leave or return?"

"I didn't see him, but I heard his damn car. I woke up and looked at the clock, and it was a quarter to two in the morning."

Coulter, the alibi-friend, had claimed Dagen left his house around one, which gave Dagen time to meet Zena at the butte or even pick her up and take her there. Jackson thanked Peggy, then crossed the street to knock on more doors, but he didn't find anyone home.

As he climbed back into his sedan, Lammers called and, as usual, cut right to the chase. "The standoff is over, and our team is fine. No casualties, except for the shooter." Her voice wavered at the end, and the sergeant cleared her throat. "I thought you might want an update."

"Of course. Thank you." Relief for Schak and Evans washed over him. "What about the hostages?"

"They're fine too. It looks like we caught Mitchell's killers."

"Great news." But he was confused. "So what happened? Why were there hostages?"

Lammers grunted. "I don't have time to give you a full briefing."

"I'll take the short version. All I know is that Evans got called out with the SWAT unit late last night."

"Schak found a connection between the cases Mitchell and Perkins were working," Lammers explained. "He and Quince went out to question Jorio Radovick and ended up shooting him. But a second man in the house refused to surrender."

"And the hostages?"

"Trafficked women, probably from El Salvador, an offshoot of the gang's drugs and gun trade."

"Thank goodness it's over."

"Copy that." Lammers ended the call.

Jackson sat for a moment, letting the stress run out of his body. He'd been worried, almost to the point of distraction, since Evans had run out of the department the night before. Time to let that all go and decide his next move. Maybe lunch and more coffee first.

As he started the engine, his phone rang. *Katie.* She was calling again, rather than texting. Something was going on. "Hey, Katie. What's up?"

"Kera is here packing her and Micah's stuff. She's crying, so the boys are crying. I think you need to get your ass home and deal with this."

Chapter 26

Kera's car sat in the middle of the driveway, so Jackson parked on the street, then hurried inside. From the entrance hall, he couldn't see anybody, but he heard Kera raise her voice. "Micah, that's not your toy. Put it back."

Jackson braced himself and stepped into the living room. The boys were sorting a trunk full of plastic dinosaurs, trucks, and other gadgets. Benjie ran to him and leaped into his arms. "The Legos are mine. Tell them, Daddy."

Oh boy. Jackson squeezed him tight and whispered, "Let it go. I'll buy you more."

Benjie gave him a doubtful look. Jackson nodded and mouthed *I promise.* He set Benjie down and touched Kera's grandson's shoulder. "Hi Micah."

"Hi." The boy, busy putting toys into a cardboard box, barely looked at him.

Jackson wondered where his daughter was, but apparently Katie was smart enough stay out of the fray.

Kera walked in from the hall. "Hey, Wade." Her eyes were dry, but it was obvious she'd been crying. "You really don't have to be here. I know you're busy with a case."

Jackson stepped toward her, but she made a gesture indicating they should move into the kitchen. As he followed her, he spoke softly. "There's no rush to move, unless that's your choice."

"My choice?" Her tone was harsh. "Daniel threatening to take Micah was not my choice. My son dying was not my choice. Micah's mother dying was not my choice." Her voice cracked, and tears pooled in her eyes. "But yes, I am choosing to compromise with Daniel to spare my grandson any more trauma."

Jackson's heart broke for her—but he couldn't change or fix any of it. "I'm sorry. How can I help?"

"You can't. Just let me pack and get out of here." She tried to smile and failed. "Actually, if you have a minute to supervise the boys, maybe feed them lunch, I would appreciate it."

"Of course."

Kera walked away before he could offer even a comforting touch. Jackson wondered what their life together would have been like if neither of the boys had come into it. If he and Kera had been able to spend more time alone together without all the parental stress. Would they have bonded better? Fallen more deeply in love? Or would Evans have been a factor, no matter what?

He would never know, and it didn't matter now. He had done his best with every new development in their chaotic lives, and he would handle this one too. Jackson opened the fridge and pulled out the makings for grilled-cheese sandwiches. They all needed some comfort food.

Chapter 27

Jackson drove back to the department, feeling guilty and frustrated. The trauma to Kera and the boys wasn't technically his fault, but it would have been if he'd decided to back out of the new rental a day earlier. His frustration stemmed from realizing that Zena's case might never be labeled anything but an *overdose*, just another statistic in the tragic and growing number of drug-related deaths. The pandemic year had been the worst on record, and health/safety officials would never know how many were suicides versus accidental. The abundance of illegal fentanyl was still a main contributor, but new, more-powerful synthetic opioids had recently hit the black market.

At his desk, Jackson read through his case notes and updated his task list. He kept coming back to the idea that Dagen and his mother had both been involved in Zena's death. Their conflicting timeline accounts could have been orchestrated to cover for each other. Even if they hadn't killed her directly, one or both had probably provided her with the fentanyl and encouraged her to use it, maybe even suggesting she kill herself. Zena had been a troubled, young, pregnant woman, and it might not have taken much to push her in that direction.

Still, he couldn't ignore the cult factor. Jackson was anxious to hear from Dallas, but her mission could take weeks. An image of Zena's mutilated finger popped into his mind. Jackson's belly filled with disgust. Had other children been maimed? Were they in danger now? Jove Goddard and his Simple Path bullshit had been in Eugene for decades. There had to be information somewhere. He glanced at his to-do list and saw the notation: *Find ex-cult member.*

Easier said than done. Maybe he needed to ask for public help. The thought of giving a press conference made him shudder. His second option was almost as bad, but he had no choice. Jackson took a deep breath and called Sophie Speranza, the crime-beat reporter for the local paper.

She picked up immediately. "Jackson! Good to hear from you. Have we got another crime to solve?"

We? She was so annoying! But she'd also been helpful on many occasions and apparently considered herself part of the team. "Sort of. I need information about a local cult called Simple Path. Specifically, I'd love to speak with an ex-member."

"I've never heard of it. They must be really secretive."

"That's why I need help."

"You want me to draft a story? Ask the public to come forward?"

"Yes."

"It's not a news story without a crime. You have to give me something."

He'd known she would ask and had already decided what he could share. "A young woman is dead of an overdose that might have been forced on her. She was pretty beat up, and we know she recently left the cult. We would appreciate any information people might have."

"What's her name?"

Jackson couldn't think of a reason to hold it back. "Zena Summers. But she was born Kenna Slaney and changed it when she left the cult."

"Maybe she was hiding from them." Sophie sucked in a breath. "You think another member killed her."

"It's just one theory."

"What are the others?"

"I'm not at liberty to say." Jackson wanted to get off the phone.

"I need more details. Where was her body found?"

"At the top of Skinner's Butte."

Someone in the background started talking to Sophie in an excited voice. Jackson started to end the call.

"Hey, I just got word about a police standoff in West Eugene. Is that connected to Officer Mitchell's murder? My new boss really wants an update."

"Yes, and we got the killer."

"Tell me more!"

"If you get the cult-information request into tomorrow's edition, I'll give you an exclusive."

"Deal."

Chapter 28

Saturday, 6:15 p.m.

As the gate opened and she followed Augie's truck through, Dallas grinned. She was already inside her target group, her fastest work yet. But the hard part was just getting started. If someone had killed the defector girl on behalf of the cult and its secrets, the believers would close ranks around that person. The most she could hope to accomplish was to figure out who did their dirty work, then let Jackson take it from there. That was a best-case scenario. Her mission would be more challenging if a member had committed the murder for personal reasons.

The metal clanged closed behind her, and a wave of apprehension flowed through her gut. Being on the inside was always a little nerve-racking, and she didn't know the code to open the gate and get out. *Yet.* Dallas laughed it off. In an emergency, she could abandon the rental car and scale the wall or run into the woods on the back side of the property and make her way around. As long as they didn't have any underground bunkers where they held people captive . . .

Ahead, the asphalt ended, and the road split into three gravel lanes. The two on the sides led into housing tracts with cramped cookie-cutter dwellings. The middle lane opened into a gravel parking area surrounding a large two-story building that featured only a few narrow windows. *The community center,* she guessed, *where they met for their daily dose of programming.* The compound reminded her of the preppers. Except that community had been more rural, heavily armed, and intent on global destruction.

Augie drove around the main building, and she followed him to a large home behind it. It probably belonged to their leader, who of course lived in a nicer place and drove a better car—if that new BMW was his. Dallas parked next to it and climbed out. This might be her toughest moment: meeting the egomaniac in charge. If he distrusted or disliked her for any reason, she would be out.

Augie took her hand. "Don't be nervous. He's always in a good mood after dinner."

For a second, she felt like a high school kid meeting her boyfriend's father. The thought almost made her laugh. As a teenager, that scenario had never intimidated her. Having parents who went on long benders of drug and alcohol use made other kids' parents seem like saints and pushovers. This would be neither.

Augie knocked on the door, smiled at her, then rocked on his heels as he waited.

He was nervous.

After a moment, he leaned toward the door and yelled, "It's Augie."

A voice boomed back, "Well, get in here."

Augie pushed open the door, and they stepped inside. The simplicity of the home surprised her. Spacious, for sure, but it had no fancy trimmings or expensive finishes and was bright with natural daylight from the horizontal windows at the top of the walls. Complete privacy without feeling cave-like. *Unusual.*

Dallas spotted a built-in rectangular cabinet the shape of a 52-inch flatscreen, but there were few other furnishings. The man who walked toward them was six-three, with sandy hair and a muscular body. And quite handsome. He had large hazel eyes, a strong jawline, and perfect facial symmetry.

Augie shifted his feet. "Jove, this is my new friend Amber. The one I told you about."

Dallas gave him a shy smile.

"Amber, this is my dad, but we all call him Jove."

His father! A bonus. She would have more access to the inner circle. Dallas held out her hand to shake, then said, "Unless you'd prefer not to." Since the pandemic, a lot of people had stopped touching strangers.

He grabbed her hand with both of his and squeezed. "Physical contact is what makes us human—and happy. Welcome."

A charmer. Most cult leaders were. "Thank you. I'm delighted to be here."

"Augie tells me you're in transition. I hope we can lead you in the right direction."

"I could use the guidance."

"Then you're in the right place." Jove pivoted to Augie. "Have you eaten?"

"Yes. Thanks."

"Good. I need a little more time to prepare for tonight's inspiration. Get your friend settled in, and I'll see you later in the meeting hall." Jove put his hands together in front of his chest. "Harmony is love."

Augie did the same. "Harmony is love."

Back outside, Augie said, "I'll leave my truck here and walk. Follow me in your car, so we can unload some of your stuff."

Also unusual. But it was a short trip down a gravel lane to a house that matched all the others. The cottages, 800-square-feet or so, had no garages and narrow front lawns that were brown from the long summer.

"Just park in the yard," Augie instructed.

Dallas pulled off, grabbed her overnight bag, and got out. The housing reminded her of army barracks built back in the fifties.

"I used to live in Jove's big house and just moved back here recently," Augie said, opening the door. "I know this place is small, but it has everything I need."

Dallas hoped for two bedrooms or a comfortable couch. She planned to stall on having sex with Augie, get what she needed, and get out. If it became necessary to give someone a blowjob to accomplish her goals, Jove was a better target. Her boyfriend wouldn't approve, but Cam would never know. She couldn't let puritanical social norms get in the way of her work. Lives were always at stake, and in this case, those at risk were children. Maybe women too.

To help them, she needed either witness testimony or access to incriminating files. Because the cult didn't have cell phones and personal computers she could hack, this job would be harder and require mostly old-school methods. Still, she couldn't believe the compound didn't have *any* phone or internet access. Cult leaders and preachers rarely held themselves to the same standards as their followers. Jove probably crafted his "inspirations" on a computer like everyone else. If necessary, she would find it and access it.

Augie squeezed her around the shoulders. "The second room is full of my stuff and doesn't have a bed, but you can put your clothes in there and sleep on the couch."

"Okay." Dallas glanced around. A tidy space with a mini-kitchen off to the side, all rather claustrophobic. Good thing she planned to be loaded during the evenings she spent here. She wanted to get started on that soon. The beer she'd consumed that afternoon hadn't fazed her. But she hadn't eaten since breakfast, and her stomach growled loud enough for Augie to hear.

"Oh, sorry. I forgot that you didn't eat lunch with me earlier." He moved toward the fridge. "Do you like eggs? We have chickens, so I have plenty."

"Scrambled, with cheese?" Dallas scooted in behind him and peered over his shoulder. "Got any beer in there?"

"Oh darn. I forgot to pick up some on the way home."

"I have vodka in my bags somewhere. It's leftover from a party earlier this summer." She pushed her breasts against him briefly, then stepped back. "We should celebrate."

"Yeah. A fresh start for both of us."

An hour later, they sat on folding metal chairs in the community room. Dallas had just enough buzz to make the message, whatever it was, slightly more tolerable. Augie, though, was borderline drunk on one shot of vodka. She hoped he didn't get sloppy or make a public scene. Jove might send her packing if he thought she was corrupting his son.

About fifty people filled the room, mostly women of all ages. A few had male partners and children with them, but not many. Dallas wondered where the rest of the members were. Her research indicated a hundred or so lived behind the wall. She leaned over and whispered, "Is this the whole community?"

"No. A lot of members work nights, and women with children only have to attend twice a week."

"Who's that?" She nodded toward a man who stood near the doors, as if taking a silent roll call. He was dark-haired, muscular, and forty-something.

"Uncle Craig. He's our handyman and Jove's overall assistant."

The enforcer, Dallas thought. She glanced back at Augie. "I hope this meeting isn't too religious."

Augie laughed softly. "Not at all. Most of us are atheists."

That didn't mean the message wasn't "religious." But she was curious.

"Good evening!" Jove's voice boomed from the front. "What do we say?"

"A simple life is a good life!" the members echoed back.

Typical, Dallas thought. Cults thrived on the power of shared language and rituals.

Next he asked everyone to sing, which they cheerfully did, accompanied by a woman at a piano. The lyrics included references to love, sharing, and living in harmony with each other and nature. *Harmless, so far.*

Jove smiled widely at the group. "First, let's attend to some housekeeping matters." The leader asked for more volunteers to help harvest the last of the garden crops and to spread the gravel being delivered. "Winter is coming," he joked.

It gave Dallas a chill.

The meeting transitioned into a lecture about the importance of commitment to the community and "forsaking" a focus on "one's own personal needs."

Jove's tone brightened, and he launched into a ramble about how "special" the Path and its members were. "We have a secret knowledge that keeps us safe and gives our lives transcendent purpose."

Those key words, *special* and *secret*, were the honey, the lure that pulled people into cults and kept them there.

Nothing new or alarming so far. Dallas tuned out for a few minutes, thinking about her first objectives: seek out Zena's mother, then get access to membership records.

A moment later, Jove said something that made her sit up straighter.

"The future is apocalyptic for those who are addicted to the internet and its easy access to gratification. That addiction leads directly to mental illness, alienation, and suicide. Trust me. I know these things about the future because I've lived in that dark place. And I've come back to save you."

What the hell?

Chapter 29

A few hours later

Dallas retrieved the bottle of vodka she'd stashed in the freezer and sat back on the couch. She scooted close to Augie and leaned her head on his shoulder. So far, he hadn't told her much, but he was drunk enough now to get sloppy. He'd sobered up somewhat during the crazy two-hour Path meeting, then they'd started drinking again soon after. But first, Dallas had taken five minutes in the bathroom to key some hurried notes into her phone while they were still fresh in her mind. Jove Goddard was a scammer right up there with L. Ron Hubbard, who'd founded Scientology. She was still puzzled by what was in it for Jove, other than the power trip. None of his followers seemed to have any money, or maybe they'd given it all to him.

Augie kissed her forehead. "You're so pretty. And sweet."

He'd never seen her in action with a sniper rifle.

"I like you too." She let him kiss her, then whispered in his ear. "We're still getting to know each other." Dallas poured more vodka into his orange juice and took a small sip straight from the bottle. "I met your father, but where is your mother?"

Augie shrugged. "I don't know. She abandoned me."

"That's sad, but at least you had one parent."

"Sort of." He was quiet for minute. "But you're right. I am lucky." He sounded slurry but a little rote. "Jove and his teachings kept me from trashing my brain with video games and social media."

"You grew up here from a young age?"

"Yeah." He gulped his screwdriver and wiped his mouth on his sleeve.

"What was it like? Most communes like this are pretty laid back and unstructured. I would've loved that as a kid."

Augie let out a harsh laugh. "Until you went into the penalty box."

What? That sounded creepy. "What does that mean?"

"Never mind. I'm just drunk." He giggled. "Why'd you get me so shit-faced?"

"We're just partying." She planned to snoop around for the *box* later. Dallas rubbed his leg. "Do you ever think about leaving? Just curious." She wanted to ease the conversation toward Zena. Maybe ask about others who'd left.

"I used to." A deep sadness in his tone.

"What happened?"

"Too much to talk about." He leaned his head on her shoulder. "Getting a job on the outside"—he paused to burp—"and going to the bar helped me feel more settled here for a while."

"Other kids who grew up here left though, right?"

"A few. I'm the oldest of the kids born in the compound." His head rolled back against the couch.

Was he passing out? Dallas squeezed his leg. "Hey, we're still celebrating and talking."

"Okay." Augie forced his eyes open.

"Do you have friends here? I'd like to meet them." Dallas laughed and pretended to slur her words. "Later, I mean."

After a long moment, Augie said, "My best friend just left."

"I'm sorry. What's his name?"

"Her name is Kenna."

Zena's birth name. Did he know she was dead? "Is her family still here? Are they okay with her leaving?"

Augie's head rolled back again. "It's just her mom and brother. They both miss her."

"What's her mother's name?" A second later, *Pearl* popped into her head. Dallas had seen it on the birth certificate scan Jackson had sent. The alcohol was making her a little slow.

"Pearl. She lives by the garden." His words came slowly.

"I love gardens. Let's go see it first thing in the morning. Okay?"

Augie didn't respond.

Dallas glanced over. His eyes were closed. She waited five minutes, then began to search.

Bedroom first. A narrow bed, a beat-up dresser, and an old trunk filled the small space. Dallas searched the drawers first, finding only clothing, most of it rather threadbare and stained. Hooks on the wall held a pair of black pants and two kelly-green pullovers. *His work uniform*, she guessed. No closet. These tiny homes had been built by a minimalist with no wasted space.

Dallas dropped to the floor and peered under the bed. Shoes and dust.

In the trunk, under a winter jacket, she found a skateboard, a few books, and a basketball. Did the compound have hoops, maybe some concrete for activities? She pulled out the toys, hoping to find paperwork or a birth certificate, even though Augie wasn't her real target. Jove was the person with secrets, the one who had the most to gain by silencing ex-cult members like Zena. But getting to him, with or without seduction, would take longer.

Did she have time? Augie's mention of a "penalty box" for children had been disturbing.

On the bottom of the trunk lay a pale-yellow folder. After a quick glance over her shoulder, Dallas opened it. Inside were photos, some Polaroid, some standard prints. Most were of Augie as a child. His cute, little-boy face with dimples had matured into adulthood without changing much. The last image in the stack caught her attention. A woman, maybe twenty-five, sitting in a rocker, holding a baby. She had the same hair color and dimples as Augie, but she wasn't smiling. The mother who'd abandoned him?

Chapter 30

Months earlier

Kenna woke to the sound of a rooster crowing, opened her eyes, and instantly thought, *This is the day!* She'd been eager for her eighteenth birthday for so long she'd started to feel like time had stopped. But it was finally here, and she was leaving this place. She quickly got up and got dressed, then glanced at her younger brother Ben sleeping in the other single bed. She would miss him . . . and her mother, but it was time to leave. Time to live!

She'd packed her few belongings the night before and had strongly considered leaving then—but she didn't know the code to the gate. It wasn't the only way out though. The wall wasn't closed at the top of the property, and she'd wandered outside the perimeter a few times over the years. Yet she'd never considered running away. Jove and her mother would've found her and brought her back, then made others suffer for it. She also hadn't had any money or any idea where to go or what to do. The world out there was such an unknown, and it terrified her even now—but she wouldn't let that stop her.

Her mother had finally accepted that she was leaving and had offered to drive her into town this afternoon when she went to work. So she planned to wait until then, hoping her mother would give her some cash. Kenna wanted to leave on good terms—despite how much she resented her mother for the choices she'd made. She loved Pearl dearly, but she would never forget, or forgive, what she'd suffered as a child—and a teenage girl—in this crazy place. One of the first things she planned to do on the outside was change her name. She didn't trust Pearl or Jove to leave her alone and not pressure her to return, at least for social gatherings.

A shiver ran up her spine. Did she trust Jove to actually let her go? Kenna had wanted to keep her departure a secret, but her mother had known it was coming for years, and Pearl's loyalty was to Jove, always.

"Zena Summers." She said her chosen name out loud, hoping to feel stronger. She would need to be a warrior to survive on her own, to find an apartment and a job. Kenna was the past, and she would think of herself as Zena from this moment forward. Someday, she would find her father too, but that was down the road and might take years.

After dressing in her favorite clothes, Zena scooted into the kitchen to make tea and breakfast. She still had some things to take care of and a few people to say goodbye to.

"Good morning." Ben shuffled into the kitchen. "What are you making?"

"Peanut butter pancakes, your favorite."

"Yay!" He sat at the table, still yawning. "It's not Sunday. Are we celebrating something?"

It was time to tell him. Zena had been putting this off, hoping to find a way around it. She wanted to take him with her, but she had no idea how to make that work. Even if they could hide from anyone who came looking, how would she take care of him? She would probably have to sleep on the streets for a while. Zena shut down that line of thinking.

She'd gone over it in her head a million times. She promised herself she would come back for Ben when she had the necessary resources.

"This will be our last breakfast together for a while." Zena smiled and tousled his hair. "I'm an adult now, and I need to find a job. I plan to get an apartment in town too."

"You're moving out?"

"I have to." As a boy, his experience here would never be as bad as hers, thank goodness, but she would spare him those details. At nine, he was too young to understand anyway. Zena leaned in and whispered, "I'll come back for you soon, but you can't tell anyone that."

Ben nodded. "Mom too? Can we all go live somewhere else?"

Zena shrugged. "Pearl does what she wants."

After breakfast, Ben asked her to play cards with him. "And finish our puzzle," he added.

Zena was glad for the distraction. Her mother wouldn't leave for work until three, so Zena had time to kill before her ride into town. Where was Pearl this morning? She was probably at Jove's or Craig's, but maybe she hadn't even come home. Sometimes the adult parties lasted all night.

After she and Ben played cards for nearly an hour, they pulled up the tablecloth and started working on the puzzle underneath.

A few minutes later, the door burst open, and Jove stepped in.

Zena froze, and Ben's eyes went wide.

"Why aren't you both working on the wall?" His voice was eerily calm.

Zena stood. "This is my last morning with Ben. I thought—" She stopped. No point in explaining.

"Not doing community chores is a serious infraction." Jove was even quieter now.

Zena's heart began to pound. Would he try to detain her?

"Ben, come with me." Jove grabbed her brother's arm.

"No!" Zena jumped up. "This is my fault. I'm the one who got distracted." *Where the hell was her mother?* Not that she would be much help.

"I should put you in the penalty box too, but you're eighteen now, so your punishment will be that of an adult."

No! Her heart pounded so hard her chest hurt. "I'm not a member anymore, and I'm leaving today. Just let this go, please."

Jove's icy blue eyes locked on hers. "You'll always belong to Simple Path." He spun toward the door, dragging Ben.

Zena rushed out after them, totally panicked. She couldn't physically stop this. Jove was too big, and Craig was always lurking somewhere nearby, ready to step in. He'd been a nice man long ago, but this place had changed him. Poor Ben stumbled along behind Jove, whimpering, but too confused and limited to object.

Zena could only follow. Their neighbor, Isabelle, watched from her window, but didn't intervene. Gravel crunched beneath their feet as they all hurried down the path to Jove's home. Zena tried to calm herself but couldn't. Ben had been left in the penalty box once before, and it had traumatized him. He didn't have the intellectual capability to think ahead and tell himself it would eventually end. Zena had spent a lot of time in there and had learned to zone out for hours at a time, but Ben . . .

The box wasn't even her worst fear. The "adult" punishment Jove had mentioned made her so nauseous she felt like throwing up.

Run! The thought overwhelmed her. Ben was going into the box no matter what. But if she ran, Jove might leave him there for days to make her feel responsible. Or worse.

Jove dragged Ben through the gate into his backyard and stopped in front of a square metal structure. Zena caught up to him and pleaded, "I'll take the punishment, whatever it is, just let Ben go."

What was she saying? Jove might lock her in there and never let her out. *No.* That wasn't what he had in mind. A vivid scene played in her brain, and Zena flinched as she remembered Craig cutting off the tip of her finger. She'd later come to understand that had been his punishment—and how Jove controlled people.

He opened the shed, shoved Ben inside, and slammed the door. But he didn't lock it . . . yet. Jove turned to her, his handsome face smiling but his eyes cold. "It won't be that bad," he said softly. "This is your first infraction as an adult."

Could she reason with him? "Technically, I'm not eighteen until seven this evening."

Jove scowled. "How do you know that?"

Zena wanted to bite off her tongue. She'd seen the time on the birth certificate she'd stolen from her mother's file case. "Pearl told me."

He seemed to accept that.

"Can you please let this go? Ben is handicapped, and I'm almost out of here. But I'll work on the wall until I leave."

Jove silently opened the shed door. "Either step inside and be an adult or forget about leaving. You can't have it both ways."

Hatred burned so hot in her heart, she almost lunged at him, but that would be a mistake. Not only was he too big to take down, other members would punish her. "What is it? What do I have to do?"

"Ben's hands were idle when they should have been working." Another toxic smile. "So a small fracture in one of his fingers seems appropriate."

Zena's stomach roiled, and her breakfast lurched into her mouth. She bent over and vomited. As she straightened up, Jove grabbed her wrist and squeezed so hard she thought he'd broken a bone. He yanked her in close and bent down so his face was inches away from hers. "Get used to it. Your retarded little brother will never leave this compound, and if you ever do or say anything that comes back to hurt me or the Path, I will punish Ben. Understood?"

Chapter 31

Sunday, Oct. 4, 4:15 a.m.

Dallas opened her eyes and, for a moment, wondered where the hell she was. *Oh yeah.* Augie's bed, inside the Path compound. He'd fallen asleep on the couch, so she'd crashed in here after setting her internal alarm to wake up in a few hours. She sat up, scowling at her slight headache. Dallas swung her feet to the floor, then pulled on her jeans and running shoes. She wanted to get outside and explore the compound before anyone got up. Augie would show her around later, but his tour might be too selective.

She downed a glass of water, then grabbed a lightweight jacket from her overnight bag. She started to pocket a mini-flashlight, but changed her mind. Might as well take the burner phone in case she wanted to snap pictures of anything useful or incriminating.

After tucking it into her front pocket, Dallas stepped outside. The cold air was unexpected. *So unlike Phoenix.* The stillness was unfamiliar too. No traffic sounds. Nobody moving around. No street lights. Fortunately, a full moon gave her some visibility.

Dallas instinctively ran along the lane toward the community center, her footsteps crunching on the gravel. She quickly veered off and kept to the front yards. She wanted another look at Jove's house, coming up on the left, his fenced backyard in particular. A row of trees separated his property from the cottages, but she wasn't intimidated. As she darted toward the oak tree in the middle, a car engine fired up, startling her. Dallas ducked behind a tree and waited until the vehicle sounds faded in the direction of the exit. Probably someone going to work in a bakery or a hospital. She was relieved to know that some members regularly opened the gate and left the compound.

The thick tree proved challenging to climb, but she managed to get high enough to see over Jove's back fence. The large yard held a greenhouse, a chicken coop, and a tool shed between the two. Nothing particularly sinister. In the dark, she couldn't tell for sure, but the shed looked padlocked.

Dallas sensed movement and shifted her gaze to the lane on the other side of Jove's property. A woman, braced against the cold, was moving quickly. *Had she just left Jove's home?* Dallas shimmied down from the tree and hurried after her.

Keeping off the noisy gravel, she jogged along the dormant grass again. The woman turned down a secondary lane heading west, and Dallas followed her to the end. Beyond the cottages were rows of withering corn. Was this Zena's mother? Augie had said Pearl lived by the garden.

The woman stopped and stared into the field, mountains rising in the distance. A moment later, Dallas heard sobbing. Grieving for her daughter?

She crossed into the lane and hurried toward the woman, letting her footsteps be heard. The woman turned, startled. She was quite pretty, despite her watery eyes, and her thin dress revealed the curves of her slender body. *Was she Jove's mistress? Doing an early morning walk of shame?*

"Are you okay?" Dallas spoke softly, showing concern.

Her tears kept rolling. "Who are you?"

"Amber, a friend of Augie's. What's your name?"

"It doesn't matter."

Dallas moved in close and gave her a shoulder hug. "Do you live around here? Can I make you some hot tea?"

The woman tried to get control, but she shivered from the cold as well as her trauma.

"Let's get you inside," Dallas soothed. "Is that your house?"

She nodded, and Dallas steered her toward the front door.

Once inside, Dallas heated water in the electric tea kettle on the counter, then grabbed a sweater from a hook and handed it to the shivering woman. She pulled it on, mumbled, "Thanks," and plopped on an old couch.

"Tell me your name."

"Pearl." Her sobs had settled, but the tears kept flowing. "I'm sorry. I just hadn't let myself grieve until now." She sounded high on something. Obviously, partying wasn't against the rules here.

"Who are you grieving for?"

"My daughter Kenna." Another round of sobs.

Dallas patted her shoulder. "I'm so sorry for your loss."

The tea kettle whistled, so she got up and made two cups of Lipton, the only kind she found in the sparse cupboards.

As Pearl sipped her tea, Dallas gently probed. "What happened to Kenna?"

"An overdose. She left Simple Path, but it clearly didn't make her happy."

"Why did she leave?"

"She wasn't happy here either." A long pause. "That's probably my fault. I'm not a good mother." Pearl's face tightened in self-hatred.

Dallas concurred, but wanted to say something supportive. "You let her go. That seems like the right thing."

Pearl nodded. "I even took her to my sister's so she'd have a place to stay. And I hadn't spoken to my sister in years."

Dallas made a mental note. Before she could ask another question, Pearl started coughing, a hacking sound that alarmed her. *Was she sick?* Dallas got up and brought her a glass of water. Pearl gulped some, then abruptly vomited on the floor.

Oh brother. Dallas stood again to fetch a dustpan or whatever she could find.

Suddenly, a young boy padded into the room.

Pearl yelled, "Go back to bed!" then looked up at Dallas. "I'm fine now. You need to leave."

Dallas stood, taken aback by her mood shift.

"Harmony is love," Pearl mumbled.

Chapter 32

Sunday, 9:50 a.m.

Schak sat in the conference room, drinking his third cup of coffee. After yesterday's standoff, he'd spent hours writing reports, then finally went home to crash. But ten hours of sleep had left him feeling sluggish and irritable. This meeting was essential though. He had to update both taskforce teams before Lammers put him on administrative leave for the "officer involved shooting." Maybe she would delay it. Quince had put bullets into Radovick too, and the Violent Crimes Unit couldn't afford to have them both sit out right now.

Quince stepped into the room and clapped him on the shoulder. "Are you okay?"

"I'm good." They had both stayed at the hostage house until the second perp was carried out on a stretcher. He was still alive, but barely. Schak nodded at Quince. "You?"

"Tired, but feeling good about our initial contact and how it all went down." Quince sat across from him. "But you made the connection. This is your moment." Quince held up his coffee in a toast.

Schak reluctantly lifted his as well. He was pleased with himself, but he didn't really need the attention. "Evans too," he added. "She pulled off a great save. Along with the whole hasty team."

Lammers strode in and sat at the end of the table. "Chief Owens wanted to be here"—she made a snarky face—"but it's Sunday morning, so it's just us. We'll keep it brief." She glanced back and forth between Schak and Quince. "Technically, you both have to go on leave, but I'll take my time filing the paperwork."

"Thank you," Schak said. "I still need to follow up on some phone records for the overdose victim." He hesitated. "After this meeting, I'd like to question Dominick Bulgar again. We need to see if he'll place Radovick at the scene of Mitchell's shooting."

Lammers gave him a look. "Even if he won't, I'm sure we've got our cop killer."

Schak nodded. "What about the women?"

"Social Services is taking care of them," Lammers said. "Three had paid Radovick to transport them across the border and arrange domestic work positions, but the employment hadn't come through, and they feared they would be sold overseas."

"What about the girl who was locked up?" Schak asked.

"She says she was snatched off the street in Chula Vista, just south of San Diego."

Schak was glad the perps were dead or dying.

"Is she okay?" Quince asked.

"Physically, yes. She declined medical treatment." Lammers' expression was grim. "They're all in a women's shelter for now, and the department will get their statements when they're ready."

That didn't answer the questions of how they'd been treated or whether they'd been sexually assaulted, or how quickly they would be deported. Schak didn't want the details. He'd seen and heard enough. But he did want to know more about the second officer's shooting. "Has anyone questioned Perkins?"

"I did." Lammers' expression softened. "I had to do something useful while you guys were out there facing armed cop killers." She glanced down at her notepad. "Perkins says he and Mitchell questioned Bulgar about Radovick after a different young woman reported being trafficked by him, then disappeared."

"Does Radovick have any other connection to Bulgar?" Schak asked.

"Go ask him." Lammers nodded. "Well done, by the way. The entire department is grateful."

At the jail, a female deputy escorted Schak to a closet-sized room on the second floor and told him to wait. Ten minutes later, a male deputy brought Bulgar in. Handcuffed and dressed in green scrubs, the inmate seemed diminished compared to their last encounter. He sat meekly at the folding table.

"Want me to stay or wait outside?" the deputy asked.

"Wait outside." Schak didn't want Bulgar to have any distractions.

After the deputy left, Schak said, "You know you're being recorded, correct?"

"Of course." Bulgar rolled his eyes. "They watch us pee in here too."

An exaggeration. Schak jumped straight to the main question. "How well do you know Jorio Radovick?"

"That's not how you pronounce it."

"Huh. So you do know him."

Bulgar shrugged. "Maybe."

"Cut the bullshit! I don't have the time or patience for games. What's your connection to him?"

"He's my cousin. Why?"

"When was the last time you saw him?"

Something clicked in the inmate's eyes. "Is he dead?"

Schak was torn about how much to reveal. He wanted the truth about what happened to Officer Mitchell, but he also wanted to close the case and go out with a win. "Very dead."

Bulgar nodded. "He was at my house Thursday morning when I was arrested."

"Why didn't you say so the last time I questioned you?"

"He's my cousin. We don't rat on each other." Bulgar sat up straighter, looking less worried. "But he's dead so it doesn't matter now."

"Does he own a rifle?"

"He has many weapons and likes to hunt, so probably." His tone was almost cocky now.

Prick! Even if Radovick had been the one who shot Mitchell, Schak couldn't let this thug walk out of jail after serving only thirty days on a probation violation. "Do you know Manny Kronin?"

"Never heard of him."

Schak decided to push this guy. "We interviewed the girls Radovick trafficked, and they described a third man who looked just like you." An easy lie.

Bulgar pretended to be surprised. "I don't know what you're talking about."

"We raided his house last night and found the victims. That's how he ended up full of bullet holes."

"I'm glad you saved those girls. I would never be involved in anything like that." He sounded sincere.

Schak didn't buy it, but the trafficking crime wasn't his case. "Why was Radovick at your house Thursday morning?"

"He stopped by to borrow some tools."

"Where was he when Mitchell showed up to arrest you?"

"Out back, rummaging through my shed for a post-hole digger."

A specific detail. He was either telling the truth or was a skilled liar. With drug users, you could never tell. "Do you keep weapons in your shed?"

A pause. "No."

"Why would your cousin shoot a police officer? Mitchell was only there to pick you up on a parole violation." Schak was curious about what he would say. His own theory was that Bulgar had warned Radovick that cops were asking questions, so Radovick had tried to take out both officers.

Bulgar shrugged. "Jorio hates cops. They killed his father."

That was what he needed. Schak sat back, feeling confident he'd closed two major cases with one great catch.

Chapter 33

Sunday, 8:15 a.m.

Jackson took the kids out to breakfast, their usual Sunday treat, and tried to explain what was happening with their broken family situation. Katie had already moved on and admitted she was glad to have more space and quiet in their "less than glam" home. Benjie was more concerned, but he seemed relieved when Jackson promised he could visit Kera and Micah in their new place. Jackson hoped it was true.

On the way home, the sunny, blue-sky day inspired him to stop at a nearby park. The trees had turned a brilliant burnt orange, but the air was surprisingly warm. The last of the *second summer* days. Jackson wanted to relax, hang out with his children, and be a normal family guy for a while. While he played with Benjie on the swings, Katie got bored and walked the last few blocks home. After a while, Jackson got restless too. Zena's death still wasn't resolved, and he had an uneasy feeling of being sidelined. Schak, Quince, and Evans had all taken part in apprehending the cop killers and rescuing the trafficked women. All he'd accomplished the day before was to question—maybe even harass—a semi-disabled woman about her pain-medication use.

His phone beeped, and he stepped away from the swings. He had a text from Dallas, sent hours earlier, but somehow delayed until now. Jackson read the message: *Jove claims he's from the future.* The text was followed by a crazy-face icon. Cults were always a little nutty, but how could people be so gullible? Something he now asked himself every day. Fringe groups and mass hysteria were definitely on the rise.

His phone dinged with another message, also sent by Dallas early that morning: *Pearl took Zena to her sister, and Zena has a younger brother. Also heard "penalty box" as punishment.*

Dallas was moving fast!

But what did it mean? Especially *penalty box*? He usually assumed the worst and went to dark places, but he had to wait for more information and real evidence. He'd never get a search warrant without it.

As for the *sister* detail, he wanted to talk to Ruby again. Maybe she'd told the truth and was just a woman with a rental, and Pearl's sister had found her. But he needed to know for sure, especially if Ruby had lied to him, or at least hidden the whole truth. Jackson glanced over at Benjie and waved, then called Ruby, but the call went to voicemail. He would drive over this afternoon and confront her face to face. He wanted to go now, but Katie had to work a lunch shift at the restaurant, and someone had to watch Benjie. As soon as his daughter returned, he would get back to work.

At home, Jackson sat down with the Sunday paper, a pathetic version of its former self, and looked for Sophie's article. Maybe her request-for-public-help article hadn't run. So far, the department hadn't called with any tips. He found the short piece on the first page of the City section, accompanied by a photo of Zena that Sophie had apparently downloaded from Facebook. Jackson scanned the text:

The overdose death of eighteen-year-old Zena Summers might have been foul play, according to a source familiar with the matter. Her body, found at the top of Skinner's Butte, had numerous bruises and abrasions. The young woman had recently changed her name after leaving a secretive cult called Simple Path, which is now a focus of the investigation. The Eugene Police Department is asking for anyone with information about the group to come forward. To leave an anonymous message, call the department's tip line or send a text through the website.

The article listed a phone number and website, then promised an update.

Jackson rubbed his temples. He was glad the request was out there, but Sophie had spun the damage to Zena's body a little too much. Lammers would not be pleased. The sergeant thought the case was likely a suicide or accidental overdose. Also, he never used the expression "foul play."

On cue, his phone rang. *Sophie.* Jackson decided to deal with her and get it over with. "Hey, I just read your article."

"And?"

"It gets the job done. But—"

"What?"

"We both look bad if her death wasn't a homicide."

"Have you ever been wrong about a cause of death?"

Jackson had to think about it. "Not the cause, but I have been wrong about the killer."

"So let's see what kind of response we get. Meanwhile, you promised me exclusive information about the standoff."

Oh hell. "I haven't been fully briefed on that yet, but I'll call you after our next taskforce meeting."

"What about a follow-up for this case?"

Did he have anything new? Oh yeah, Dallas' weird detail. "The cult leader, Jove Goddard, claims he's from the future."

"Seriously?" Sophie laughed. "That's rich considering the group is anti-technology." A pause. "Maybe he thinks he's warning people about what could happen when AI takes over." She laughed again.

"Who knows? I'll have more for you in a few days." Jackson hoped that was true.

A few hours later, he was pacing the house, feeling unsettled. It was too damn quiet. Kera and Micah were gone, Katie was at work, and Benjie was napping. But his daughter should have been home by now. He needed her to babysit.

She showed up ten minutes later, tired and grumpy from being on her feet and not getting tipped well enough. Over her objections, Jackson promised he would be back in an hour and hurried out.

Ruby answered the door and grimaced, clearly not happy to see him. "This isn't a good time."

"We need to talk." Jackson stepped forward.

Ruby sighed and let him in. She plopped into a recliner where she had a can of soda and a book sitting nearby. Jackson was tempted to take her into the department just to shake her out of her comfort zone, but he would give her a chance to come clean.

Still standing, he got right to point. "I know you're Pearl Slaney's sister, Zena's aunt. Why did you lie about that?"

Ruby stared at her hands for a long moment. "I didn't lie. I just didn't bring it up."

"Why not?"

"Pearl and I aren't on speaking terms. She didn't even come in. She just left Kenna outside." A tear rolled down Ruby's cheek. "The girl looks so much like her mother, I knew right away who she was."

"Did you tell Zena you were her aunt?"

"No. I didn't want to have to talk about Pearl. It's too painful."

"Why?"

"She's a mess."

No kidding. "In what way?"

Another silence. Finally, she said, "Pearl's an addict and a slut—and then there's the cult."

"Were you once part of it?"

"Not really. I was drawn to the idea of minimizing our dependency on technology, but the whole thing was too weird for me." Ruby pressed her lips together. "I tried to talk Pearl into leaving, but I just alienated her instead."

"Tell me what you mean by *weird*."

Ruby let out a harsh laugh. "You mean other than Jove claiming he's from the future?" Her face tightened. "But that's not important."

"Tell me what is."

"I can't." Her voice choked with anguish.

Jackson searched her eyes, trying to decide his approach. "Are you afraid of Jove?"

A pause. "Yes and no."

"Is he capable of murder?"

"I don't know." Ruby suddenly stood, her expression dark. "I can't talk about Simple Path."

"Why not?"

"No one can. Jove ensures that."

"Does he threaten you? That's a crime, and you need to report it."

Ruby shook her head. "It's not like that. You might as well stop asking."

What did Jove have on these people? Maybe Dallas would find out. "What about Zena's baby? Do you know who the father is?"

She shook her head. "It could be anyone at the compound. They're all very promiscuous."

Sex with a minor was statutory rape. But unless he could match someone with the baby's DNA . . .

"I'm sorry I can't help you," Ruby said. "But this is making me very uncomfortable."

Too bad. "The state lab is doing an analysis of the fetal tissue. We will find the father."

"I hope you do." Ruby looked like she wanted to bolt.

Jackson remembered the blank line on Zena's birth certificate. "What about Zena's father? Do you know who he is?"

"No, but Zena was trying to find him. She sent her own DNA sample to 23andMe."

"And?"

"She wouldn't tell me the results, but it really upset her." Ruby closed her eyes, trying not to cry. "I think Zena might have killed herself."

Chapter 34

Earlier that morning

Dallas woke to the smell of coffee and deep-fried dough. She sat up, willing herself awake, and realized she was back in Augie's narrow bed. The events of the night before surfaced in vivid detail. Going out in the middle of the night, meeting and comforting Pearl, then sneaking back into the house. Augie had still been passed out on the couch, so she'd crashed in here for few more hours. Dallas glanced at the old-school clock on the dresser: *8:35 a.m.* Not that it mattered much.

She got up and crossed the hall into the kitchen. Augie stood at the stove, wearing only a pair of jeans. As she admired his lovely young body, her eyes were drawn to a scar on his upper back. Dallas eased up behind him and impulsively kissed the damaged tissue. "Good morning."

He turned and smiled. "That was nice." A blush. "Sorry about passing out."

"It's fine." She made pouty lips. "Is that a burn scar?"

"Yeah, a stupid accident." Augie reached for the coffee pot. "Want some?"

"Please. Cream if you have it, but I'll drink it either way."

He pointed at the fridge. "In there." Then spun back to the stove. "I'm making doughnuts."

Dallas took her coffee to the table and sat.

After a few minutes, he set a plate in front of her. "I just poke a hole in those pop-open, ready-to-bake biscuits, then fry 'em and roll 'em in powdered sugar."

Dallas chuckled. "I used to make these as a kid. A staple of growing up poor."

"I'm not poor," Augie corrected. "Short on cash, yes, but my life is rich in other ways."

It sounded like a programmed response. "What ways? I mean, what's the main attraction here?" She smiled. "I'm here because I like you, but why did everyone else join?" *Had she been too direct?*

"Peace of mind." Augie paused, then grinned. "The cheap rent is nice too." He gestured at her coffee and doughnuts. "Better eat up, we have work to do."

After hiking to the backside of the compound, they stopped near a section of wall that was under construction. A pile of bricks, a metal wheelbarrow, and a bag of dry mortar sat nearby. Augie had carried a bucket of water and explained the chore as they walked. "We started working on it three years ago, then had to stop for a while when our materials dried up."

"Is someone donating the bricks?" The wall had intrigued Dallas from the moment she saw it, and she wanted to know how it was funded.

"Sort of. Simple Path is part of a larger organization called Simple Earth Life, and they subsidize important projects like this."

Dallas made a mental note of the name. "Why did the funding stop for a while?"

"Jove had some ideas they disapproved of, but he backed down."

Her curiosity spiked, but he'd shut down the subject.

Augie picked up a broken-shovel handle. "Let's get going. I owe two hours." He dumped mortar and water into the wheelbarrow and used the broken handle to mix it. Then he demonstrated how to apply the "mud" and stack the bricks.

After a few minutes of working, Dallas casually asked, "If I needed to make an important call, is there a phone somewhere? Or would I have to go into town and find a public phone?" *Was there still such a thing?*

"Do you need to?"

"Not right now, but I will later. I'm also curious about how you get by without a laptop. I mean for things like creating a resume or sending PDFs."

"There's a landline and a computer in the community center," Augie said, laughing. "We're not Amish. But internet access is limited." He grabbed another brick. "I'll show you around after we finish here."

Chapter 35

Sunday afternoon

Back in his sedan, Jackson considered his options. He needed to get inside the compound and question everyone, but the locked gate was a problem. So was his lack of tangible evidence. Without it, a judge would never sign a search warrant.

Could he get Zena's mother to voluntarily talk to him? He had to try.

Jackson texted Katie and asked her to watch Benjie for another hour. He hoped she wouldn't resist, because he didn't plan to turn around. As he drove west, he mulled over the new information. Did it change anything? He'd already known Zena was pregnant before she left the cult, but the possibility that adults were having sex with minors escalated his concern for the children out there. It also made him swing back to the theory that the baby's father could be the killer, or at least a sexual predator.

He would call the state lab Monday morning and pressure them to expedite the fetal DNA analysis. Maybe the father was in the federal database. He would also contact the ancestry business Zena had used and see if they would send him her results. *Had they mailed her a paper copy?* If so, someone had taken it. The missing journal seemed more important than ever.

As he neared the turn onto Louis Lane, Jackson wondered if he should have asked someone to accompany him. But Schak, Quince, and Evans had all been at the standoff yesterday—after working through the night before. They needed a day off.

A few minutes later, he pulled up in front of the compound's gated entrance. The expansive wall now seemed more ominous. Jackson pressed the buzzer and waited. No response. He pressed it again. And again.

Nothing.

He climbed back in his vehicle, and called Ruby, not expecting her to answer either.

But she did, sounding weary. "Yes?"

"I need to talk to Pearl, but I can't get anyone at the compound to respond. How can I reach her? Does she have a phone?" He didn't think so, because of the cult's anti-technology founding, but maybe someone out here did.

"No. Jove is very strict about that." Ruby hesitated. "Pearl works nights at the Applebee's on Eleventh, waiting tables. You can talk to her there."

Well damn. That surprised him. Jackson kicked himself mentally for not asking the question earlier. "What time is her shift?"

"Soon. I think she starts at four or five."

"Thanks." He hoped to catch her before she even went inside. "What does Pearl look like?"

"An older version of Zena. Dark-strawberry blonde, light-brown eyes, and a cupid face." Her voice pitched upward with stress. "Please don't mention that I told you where to find her. Things are bad enough between us."

Jackson checked his phone for the time: *3:32. Perfect.* He turned around, drove to the restaurant, and parked on the side.

After a fifteen-minute wait, an old Dodge Neon pulled in near him. The driver who got out matched Ruby's description. Jackson hustled over to intercept her. "Pearl Slaney?"

The woman looked up, startled. "Not now." She held up a hand. "I have to work."

Jackson quickly identified himself. "This will only take a few minutes. Isn't your daughter's murder important to you?"

"Murder?" A wave of pain crossed her face. "I was told she overdosed."

"Who said that?"

Pearl shook her head, her mouth tight.

As long as he had her rattled, Jackson asked, "Who's the father of Zena's baby?"

"What?" Another wave of shock in her eyes.

Her mother hadn't known. "She was pregnant when she left the cult."

"We're not a cult." Her tone was beaten-down.

"What about Zena's father? Who is he?"

"Why does it matter?" Pearl cinched her sweater tighter, as though she were cold, despite the warm afternoon.

"It probably doesn't matter, but humor me."

Pearl sighed. "He's an ex-cult member and has never had anything to do with Zena." Pearl tried to maneuver around him. "I have to get to work."

Jackson blocked her. "I think you know who impregnated Zena. Not reporting sexual abuse of a minor is a crime."

"She's dead. Let it go." Pearl scurried toward the restaurant.

Chapter 36

Sunday evening

Dallas sat across the dinner table from Jove, braced for intense questioning. But the man took his time, plying her with beef kabobs and red wine, while telling stories about Augie. After filling her glass a third time, he asked, "What brings you to our community, besides my handsome son?"

"A new focus." She tightened her mouth, trying to look shameful. "I let social media run my life and determine my self-worth for too long. It almost broke me. I love the idea of giving it up."

"It's harder than you think." Jove glanced at Augie. "When you grow up without that contact connection, there isn't much temptation."

"I want to try," Dallas said, smiling. "The simple life suits me."

Jove nodded. "What about your family? Are they here in town?"

He probably appealed to, and targeted, loners. "My parents are in the Midwest. They got sucked into the whole Q-Anon thing, and eventually they turned on me." Dallas knew she was walking a fine line. She wanted to seem appropriately gullible, maybe a little paranoid, but not mentally ill. "I mean, I don't trust the government either. Or big tech companies. They're all spying and manipulating us. But the whole lizard-people idea was too much for me."

Augie reached over and squeezed her hand. Dallas worried that she'd blown it, but Jove gave her a knowing smile. "I think you'll fit in well here." He pushed his empty plate away.

What next? Dallas wondered. She hoped to get a better look at the house and backyard.

A loud knock startled all of them.

Jove quickly stood. "Excuse me." He strode to the entrance, his expression concerned.

Dallas pivoted, and as Jove opened the door, she caught sight of the man Augie had called 'Uncle Craig.'

"There's something you need to see." His voice boomed with urgency, and he held out a newspaper.

Dallas stood, wanting to get closer. "Maybe I should leave." She moved toward the living room.

After a moment, Jove thundered, "Who talked to a reporter?"

The enforcer looked grim. "I don't know. I just picked up the Sunday paper like I always do."

Augie jumped up too. "Let's go." He grabbed Dallas' arm and steered her toward the back of the house.

Behind them, Jove bellowed, "Emergency meeting. Gather everyone in the center!"

Augie rushed Dallas to the back door. "I don't want you to see this." He pushed her outside. "Go out the gate and back to my place." He closed the sliding glass door.

What was happening? Dallas desperately wanted back inside. This could be the eye-witness evidence Jackson needed for a search warrant. She gently slid the door open and listened.

Jove was ranting, but she only caught bits and pieces. " . . . violated our code of secrecy . . . no exceptions . . . shut it down."

Dallas didn't want to get caught eavesdropping, so she stepped away from the house and looked around the backyard for the gate. She might as well head for the community center, where everyone was gathering. Augie clearly didn't want her there, but she could loiter outside a window.

The gate was to her left and apparently opened into the gravel lane. The shed she'd spotted during her middle-of-the-night excursion drew her attention. She wanted to see if it was locked, and if not, check out what was inside. Dallas glanced back at the house to ensure no one was watching out the sliding door, then jogged across the scraggly grass. The sun was dropping in the sky, and the row of trees on the other side of the back fence cast long shadows—but the padlock on the shed was visible from a distance, and it was unlocked.

Dallas hurried over. As she reached for the latch, Augie called out, "What are you doing?"

She turned and hurried toward him. "Just looking for the gate. You rattled me. What's happening?"

Augie stepped outside. "Jove is on the warpath, but it's nothing for you to worry about." He grabbed her arm and walked her to the gate. "Please just wait in my house. I'll be there soon."

Dallas decided not to risk hanging around the community center. As the new person in the group, any suspicion—for whatever had happened—might naturally fall on her. It crushed her not to spy on the big meeting, but she didn't want to risk getting booted out of the compound. Or worse.

Like what? She didn't know. So far, she hadn't seen any weapons.

Dallas slow-walked up the gravel lane, noticing a woman and child hurrying out of a cottage across from Augie's. Dallas smiled, but the woman ignored her and moved rapidly in the other direction. Dallas scanned the boy as she passed, noting that he looked fine. Earlier that afternoon, she'd seen a boy, eleven or so, who was missing the lobe of his left ear. Her first thought was that a dog had bitten him—but there were no animals in the compound—and later, she'd remembered an odd detail from Jackson's case notes. Zena, the dead girl, was missing the end of a finger. Also, Augie had that burn scar. In such a small community, that many childhood injuries seemed like a peculiar coincidence. Yet the idea that members were removing chunks of flesh from children as a punishment seemed extreme for a nonreligious cult based on neo-Luddism.

Inside Augie's cottage, Dallas rushed into the bathroom and retrieved her phone from the bottom of her purse. She texted Jackson: *Cult is part of Simple Earth Life. News story triggered Jove's anger. Saw kid with missing earlobe and another with burn scar. Can't be coincidence? Hope to find out more soon.*

She sent the message, stashed the phone again, then stepped outside to see if others were headed to the meeting or talking openly about it. But the night was still. If members had rushed out to the gathering, they'd moved quickly and she'd missed seeing them. Shifting gears, Dallas took a long-overdue shower and changed into a skirt and sexy tank top.

Augie came home ten minutes later, his mood dark. He wouldn't talk about the newspaper story or the emergency meeting, except to say, "A rule was broken and someone has to pay." He grabbed the bottle of vodka from the freezer and took a long drink.

Dallas sauntered up next to him. "What can I do to make you feel better?"

"Get drunk and naked with me."

Dallas smiled and reached for the bottle.

An hour later, Augie was staggering, slurring, and sobbing about "losing Kenna." He'd only grabbed her breasts once, then seemed to forget about sex again. Next to him on the couch, Dallas tried to comfort and probe at the same time. "I'm so sorry for your loss. How did she die?"

"An overdose."

"Ze—" Dallas stopped short. She'd almost blown it. "Kenna was an addict?"

"No. Just a wonderful free spirit."

"You must have been close."

Augie burped, then slumped down. "We were planning a life together."

That was news! "She was your girlfriend?"

"My soulmate."

"Why didn't you leave with her?"

"It's complicated."

Had Jove disapproved? "You think she killed herself because she felt rejected?"

"I don't know!" Augie pulled away. "Do you have more vodka?"

"Sure do." Dallas fetched the bottle, then picked up the cannabis tincture too and slipped it into her skirt pocket.

Back in the living room, Augie stood near the small front window, staring out. Dallas put her arm around him and squeezed. "You have a lot on your mind for a young man."

"I still feel like a kid!" It came out as a cry for help. "My birth certificate says I'm twenty-one, but I don't believe it."

Dallas didn't know what to make of that. "Come sit down. Let me help if I can." She felt bad for Augie. He was obviously grieving for his girlfriend and intimidated by his father—but one of them was probably the father of Zena's baby, and maybe even her killer. She couldn't back off.

She led Augie to the couch, then poured two more screwdrivers. "Want to try a little pot? It might cheer you up."

"Sure. It can't hurt." Augie's eyes were closed.

Dallas squeezed a little sativa into his drink. She hoped it would make him chatty. "Tell me about Kenna. It might help to talk about her."

"She was so curious about everything. She really wanted to see the whole world."

"I can understand that, especially after growing up in this small community."

"She hated the last few years." Augie was still slurring his words, but his anger and grief were mellowing.

"Then why would she commit suicide after finally getting out?"

After a long silence, Augie burst into tears. "If we hadn't done the damn DNA tests, everything would have been okay."

For the baby? Dallas almost asked, then remembered that *Amber* wouldn't know about Kenna's pregnancy. "You mean the Ancestry thing? Like where you send in your spit?"

"She did 23andMe because they were faster. Kenna wanted to find her father." Augie gulped his drink. "And I wanted to find my mother."

"Of course you did." Dallas stroked his hair. "Did you locate her?"

"No." He let out bitter sound. "But I learned that Jove isn't my biological father."

Chapter 37

Dallas waited for Augie to pass out, then changed back into her black jeans. She took out her burner phone and stared at it, undecided. She wanted it with her so she could take photos if needed, but if Jove caught her in his house and tried to search her ...

What was the worst-case scenario? That he would confiscate the cell and kick her out? So far, she had no reason to fear for her safety.

Dallas tucked the phone into her front pocket, then pulled on a long dark sweater to cover the bulge. She'd chosen it at the second-hand store for just this purpose. At the last moment, she stuck her switchblade and lock-picking tools into her other front pocket. They might come in handy for any number of reasons.

She slipped out and closed the door quietly behind her, not that she worried Augie would wake up. Between the vodka and cannabis, he might sleep for ten hours. As she started across the narrow yard, she heard heavy footsteps on the gravel and froze. Dallas glanced left and saw Craig coming up the lane from the center building.

Dallas stepped back softly and retreated into the house, pulling the door closed without letting the latch click. Heart pounding, she stood near the entry listening for his movements. What was the enforcer doing out so late? Patrolling? She would have to be more careful. Dallas glanced at Augie, still snoring softly.

The crunching sounds finally faded. Dallas waited another few minutes to be safe, then slipped out again. She quickly headed left, staying off the gravel as much as possible. Still, the sound of her own footsteps seemed to reverberate in the quiet darkness. She'd run into Pearl last night and now Craig this evening. How many other members were up late? A sense that someone was watching sent a shiver up her spine—but she never let fear stop her. Dallas picked up her pace.

When she arrived at Jove's fence, she located the gate, then reached over and undid the inside latch. Dallas glanced at the house—all dark and quiet—then headed straight for the shed. The *penalty box* could be anything, anywhere, or nothing at all. But she had to check out this possibility. *Damn.* The padlock was fastened now. *But why?* It had been open earlier, and Augie claimed no one locked their doors because their community was built on trust. Plus, they felt safe from outsiders.

Dallas pulled out her phone, turned on the flashlight, and examined the device. The two-inch base felt more substantial than it looked. The biggest issue in opening it though was the number of pins. This padlock could have as many as four or five. The more pins, the longer it took. Other factors, such as the tightness of the tolerance and the bitting profile, could make a difference too. This wasn't her specialty, but she had to try.

Dallas slipped her phone back into her pocket and pulled out her tools. After glancing over her shoulder, she started to work the pins. The cold air quickly made her hands stiff, which slowed her down as she tried various picks. *Shit.* This could take a while. And she also wanted to search for Zena's journal.

Augie had mumbled something about Jove having it, right after he'd mentioned confronting Jove about his parentage. At least that's what she thought he'd said. Augie had been rather incoherent, slurring his words and nodding in and out of sleep. Still, the journal could have everything they needed to shut down this scam and maybe even arrest the killer. Dallas was starting to think it might be Augie, the likely father of Zena's baby. It was a little heartbreaking. He'd seemed like a decent young man.

She felt a pin click into place. *Yes!*

As she worked at the lock, she mentally plotted her moves. If Jove actually had the journal, he'd probably stashed it in his bedroom . . . or a closet safe. That would make her SOL. She couldn't crack a safe, nor could she search Jove's bedroom with him at home. She would have to wait until he was giving another presentation at the center or was out and about for any reason. What if that was days from now? Maybe she could create a distraction tomorrow and lure him out.

Another pin released! She would have felt encouraged about getting into the shed, but her hands were getting stiffer by the minute.

Her thoughts wandered back to the journal. Why would Jove keep Zena's diary if it contained incriminating notes? Maybe he thought he could use it to blackmail or manipulate someone else. He was obviously very controlling and a little crazy, so his motive could be anywhere along the sociopath continuum.

Frustration set in. She'd been working the padlock for eight minutes and had only released two pins. Dallas glanced over her shoulder. *Oh shit!* A light had come on in Jove's house. Pearl had left his place in the middle of the night, so something similar could be happening now. Jove was obviously a night owl.

Soft voices drifted her way.

She had to get out!

Dallas pulled her pick, shoving it into her pocket as she ran toward the fence.

Chapter 38

Monday, Oct. 5, 7:25 a.m.

On his way to work, Jackson stopped by the crime lab and dropped off the items he'd found in Zena's freezer. One item off his task list. Later, at his desk, he searched online for the business office of 23andMe. The biotech company was in Southern California, so he thought their office might not be open yet, but he made the call anyway.

A receptionist cheerfully answered, "Good morning. How can I help you?"

Jackson introduced himself, then asked to speak to the CEO.

The receptionist balked. "Uh, she's not in yet, but I can have her call you."

"Who else is available? I need someone with authority now."

"If you tell me what this is about or what you need, I can connect you with the right person."

He doubted it. "A young woman was murdered, and I'm investigating. She recently got a DNA analysis from your company, and I need to see those results."

She was quiet for a full three seconds. "Uh, I don't think we can legally release those without the client's permission, but I'll ask our lawyers."

"The client is dead."

"Then I think you need a court order."

He'd expected to hear that, but it still annoyed him. "The murdered girl's name is Zena Summers. Talk to your CEO and have her call me ASAP." Jackson put the phone down, planning to call again right after the taskforce meeting.

As he keyed updates into his case notes, his phone beeped, and he glanced at the screen. Another delayed text from Dallas: *Cult is part of Simple Earth Life. News story triggered Jove's anger. Saw kid with missing earlobe and another with burn scar. Can't be coincidence? Hope to find out more soon.*

Damn. Jove had seen Sophie's story asking for ex-members to come forward. The cult leader might destroy anything incriminating, pressure members into silence, or go deeper underground. But Dallas' report about the maimed children was more alarming. Would a judge consider this text from an undercover FBI agent enough evidence for a subpoena to enter and search the compound? They also had Zena's autopsy report, which documented the missing fingertip. He would write up the request and go see Cranston after the meeting. He checked the time. Another twenty minutes.

He searched online for *Simple Earth Life* and clicked through a series of boring, then surprising, links. The organization was a loose collection of small communities that all practiced some form of neo-Luddism. SEL was also affiliated with anti-globalism, radical environmentalism, and deep ecology—whatever that was. Digging deeper, he discovered the anti-technology movement had started in the late seventies with Ted Kaczynski, the Unabomber, and was also advocated by a radical group called MOVE.

But those were in the past. The main message of SEL was about shunning technology and living in harmony with the earth and each other. That seemed harmless enough. But Jove's community, Simple Path, had clearly taken a darker turn. Jackson clicked one more link and found an unexpected blog/podcast. Jove was preaching his message about the collapse of society, without the Simple Path label, and asking for donations—a means of funding his group without bringing attention to it.

Jackson checked the time again and jumped up. He hurriedly printed copies of his notes, gathered his paperwork, and walked over to the conference room. Evans was already there, as usual, and so was Sergeant Lammers. "Where's my coffee?" she demanded.

Before he could respond, she chuckled. "Got ya."

Whoa. The Sergeant was in a rare good mood. Either her chronic pain was under control, or her workload had eased up. Of course it had. His teammates had located and taken down the cop killer.

As he took a seat, Jackson raised his cup of cold coffee to the boss. "Good morning to you too." He glanced at Evans, who looked refreshed and springlike in a lavender blouse. As soon as this case wrapped up . . .

Quince walked in, looking dapper too. "Sorry to be late."

"You're not." Jackson smiled. "But Schak is about to be."

Lammers cleared her throat. "I'd like to get started." She looked at Evans, then Quince. "But first, I'd like to thank and congratulate both of you on a job well done. The forensics team found several weapons in Radovick's home, including a rifle that fits the type used by the perp who shot Officer Mitchell. So we've got our man."

"What about the second shooter, Manny Kronin?" Quince asked.

"He's still in critical condition and not expected to live."

Evans cut in. "You said 'fits' not 'matches.' Does that mean the techs didn't find any casings at Mitchell's scene?"

"Correct." Lammers turned her gaze to Jackson. "We need to wrap up Zena Summers' death too."

Feeling pressured, he passed out his case notes. "I'd like to follow up on a new suspect, Lisha Hammersmith. She's Dagen's mother." Jackson focused on the sergeant. "Lisha has a prescription for fentanyl, both patches and a vial of injectable. Plus, she hated Zena and wanted her out of her son's life."

"Speaking of fentanyl," Lammers shot back, "we had two more overdose deaths this weekend. Seventeen-year-olds this time. That makes forty-seven for the year, *so far*. And it's not just our area. Across the country, fentanyl is a contributing factor in most of them." She was just getting warmed up. "More than a hundred-thousand Americans overdosed last year on opioids, the highest rate on record." Her tone softened. "And I strongly suspect Zena Summers is yet another casualty in that epidemic."

Jackson knew it was possible, but he wasn't ready to write her off yet. "Zena wasn't a drug user. This wasn't an accidental overdose." He refused to be swayed by the little pouch in her freezer until he knew more about it.

"Her death could have been a suicide," Lammers countered. "She was young, pregnant, troubled, and on her own. And apparently, she had access to fentanyl in her boyfriend's home."

Lisha's missing pain patches came to mind. Jackson couldn't focus on that right now. He was more concerned about Jove Goddard and his *triggered anger* about ex-cult members.

Schak suddenly hurried in. "Sorry to be late. I was on the phone pressuring the service provider to send the damn records we need." He waved a stack of papers. "But I got them. Dagen's and Zena's both." He sat down and glanced around. "No coffee?"

Jackson ignored him. "Did you look through them, or do we need to do it now?"

Lammers stood. "That's my cue."

"Wait." Schak flipped to the third page. "I did look at Zena's calls and texts on the evening of her death. They don't have the actual messages, just the numbers. Zena was texting with someone besides Dagen." He passed the page to Evans. "Run this number and see what you get."

Using her computer tablet, Evans quickly accessed a database and keyed in the number. They all waited in silence, Lammers looking impatient.

Evans scowled. "No name associated. It's a burner phone."

Crap. But it was still significant. "Whoever communicated with her didn't want to be known."

Lammers rolled her eyes. "Not necessarily. Those phones are all that some people can afford." She headed for the door. "Close the case."

"I'm still looking into the cult," Jackson called after her. After the sergeant was gone, he updated his team with the information Dallas had sent. As Evans peppered him with questions, he checked his phone again. Another text, also delayed. *Damn.* Her texts were the only ones delayed, so the problem had to be on her end.

"Hey, I heard from Dallas again." Jackson read the message out loud. "*Augie Goddard, young member, is prob father of baby. Jove may have journal but can't get to it yet.*"

"Goddard? So he's Jove's son," Evans said.

"Most likely." Jackson nodded. "I'd love for Dallas to get ahold of Zena's journal. In the meantime, I'll try for a search warrant. I'm worried about the maimed kids out there."

"What?" Schak looked stunned.

Jackson handed him a stack of papers. "Read my updated case notes." He glanced at Quince. "If I get a judge to sign off, can you go out there with us later today or tomorrow? I need everybody on this one."

The door opened again, and the front desk officer stepped in. "I'm sorry to interrupt, but I have a citizen who's responding to your request for help. Can I bring her in?"

Chapter 39

A tall blonde woman stopped in the doorway and glanced around the table. For a moment, Jackson thought she might turn and run.

"This is Maddie Drake." The desk officer gestured for the witness to enter, and she finally did. The officer backed out and closed the door.

Jackson stood and introduced himself. "Please have a seat. We appreciate you coming forward."

"I had to." Maddie pressed her lips together and sat next to Evans, who patted her arm.

"I assume you know something about Simple Path and/or Jove Goddard." Jackson tried to sound calm and soothing, as much for himself as for her. This could turn out to be a big nothing.

"I was a member, briefly, when it first started." Maddie closed her eyes. "I wasn't in a good place then. I had just left an abusive relationship with a man who also cheated on me—and I was pregnant. Jove and the community took me in."

This was obviously difficult for her, but like with an interrogation, he and his team knew to just wait and let her talk. Jackson signaled Evans to get their witness some water.

After a moment, Maddie continued. "Things were fine at first, and for a while, I thought I was in love with Jove and we might build a life together." She shook her head. "But I soon realized he was hooking up with other members. He also started talking about being from the future and sent back to warn us. Everyone else seemed to buy into it, but I knew it was bullshit."

Jackson didn't care about that scam any more. He wanted to know about the abuse. "How did Jove treat you personally?"

"He became more and more controlling. Not just of me, but of everyone." Maddie chewed on her lower lip. "He could be physical at times too. Nothing too intense, just stuff like grabbing and holding my arms or pinching me if he thought I wasn't listening."

"What about the children in the community?" Jackson had to ask.

Maddie swallowed hard, then started to cry.

Evans came back with a bottle of water and set it down.

Their witness suddenly stood. "I don't think I can do this." She shook her head. "This is why no one ever reports him."

Jackson jumped up too. "Please don't leave. We can protect you. And we need to help those kids."

"It's not about protection." Her lips trembled.

"Then what?"

The look on her face answered his question. Jackson spoke softly. "We won't judge you. It was a long time ago, and you're trying to do the right thing now."

Maddie nodded, then blurted, "He makes everyone do something so shameful they can't report him or any of the cult's secrets without risking themselves."

The quiet rage he'd been suppressing burst open, and Jackson clenched his fists. Goddard was a manipulative sociopath, one of those slippery personality-cult criminals who brought others down to his level and got away with everything. Maybe even murder. He calmed himself and pressed forward. "Did you witness any of those shameful things?"

"Just one, but it was obvious he held something over everyone."

"Will you tell us what you witnessed?"

Maddie shuddered. "I don't know."

Jackson also wanted to know what shameful thing *she'd* done, but he wouldn't ask. Not yet. He would backtrack and let her talk about something more comfortable for a while. "How did you get involved with Simple Path?"

Maddie grimaced, clearly filled with regret. "My ex knew him." She cleared her throat. "We attended some of Jove's early lectures. I was worried about our cultural dependence on technology and how if it goes down, we can lose everything—power, communications, data. Jove was preaching about those concerns when no one else seemed to be." Maddie abruptly shook her head. "That doesn't matter now. The newspaper story mentioned that a girl, an ex-cult member, had overdosed. Do you think Jove was responsible?"

"We don't know." Jackson locked eyes on her. "Is he capable of that? I mean, either pushing her to commit suicide or actually giving her a lethal injection?"

Maddie blinked hard. "Yes to the first. He's very manipulative and likes to keep his own hands clean. So yeah, that would be his method, talking her into killing herself."

It was just an opinion, Jackson reminded himself. It wouldn't carry any weight with a judge. "Please tell us what crime you witnessed, so I can get a subpoena to enter the compound and question everyone."

Maddie sat still for a long moment, her lips pressed together. Finally, she blurted, "I saw someone burn a child." She burst into sobs. "Please don't make me talk about it."

Jackson took a long deep breath. "Will you sign a brief statement?"

Maddie nodded.

He gave her a moment to compose herself and glanced around at his team. They looked stunned—and they'd seen it all. Jackson brought his gaze back to their witness. "What does Jove hold over you?" he asked softly. "Saying it out loud could free you from that grip. We won't hold you accountable." *Could he promise that?*

"I left my child in the cult," she cried out. Still sobbing, Maddie struggled to speak, but she finally managed to say, "I gave him to Jove to raise. He couldn't have children and really wanted one. My ex didn't want the boy, and I was afraid he would look just like his father. I didn't think I could handle that."

Jackson reeled with recriminations and questions. *How could she? What child? The one Dallas had mentioned?*

Evans cut in, her tone sharp. "Is your son's name Augie?"

"I don't know." Maddie was still crying. "I named him Ari, but I'm sure Jove changed it."

"What about his biological father? Is he still in town? What's his name?" Jackson needed details for his subpoena.

"He doesn't matter anymore." Maddie abruptly stood and fled the room.

Chapter 40

Monday late morning

Sweat beaded on her forehead as Dallas laid another row of brick. She and Augie had been working on the wall for an hour, and she'd dressed too heavily. The cold morning air had quickly given way to warm sunshine, at least for the moment.

"How are you feeling?" She touched Augie's shoulder as he reached for another brick.

"Better. But I should take it easy on the drinking today." His dimpled cheeks flushed. "Sorry about being emotional last night."

"It's okay. You're still grieving."

"I told you about Kenna, didn't I?"

Dallas smiled. "She sounds like a great person."

"Don't mention her around Jove, okay?" Augie spread mortar on the brick and set it on the wall.

"He didn't like her?"

"It's complicated."

He'd also said that about why Jove didn't want him to leave with his girlfriend. *What was Augie still hiding?* "My parents hated my first boyfriend," Dallas offered. "They thought he wasn't good enough for me. So I understand."

Augie shook his head. "It's not like that, but I don't want to talk about it."

They went back to work, and Dallas racked her brain for ways to get Jove out of his house for a while. Short of injuring Augie and leaving him lying there to be rescued, she couldn't come up with anything. She would have to wait for Jove's evening inspiration, then fake not feeling well.

An hour later as they walked back down the hillside, Augie said, "We'd better hurry or we'll be late for community lunch." He picked up his pace.

Dallas hustled up next to him. "Is it mandatory?"

"Mostly. Jove likes to keep everyone connected on a daily basis, so we either gather for lunch or inspiration hour."

Jove would be there. Perfect.

Back in Augie's place, Dallas took a quick shower, then stepped into the living room where Augie waited. She held a hand to her lower abdomen. "I've got bad cramps and need to lie down." *That time of the month* could be her excuse for not having sex with him—if he pushed the issue.

"I'm sorry." His pretty face expressed concern. "You need to eat. You worked hard this morning."

"Can you bring me something?"

"Sure." He came over and kissed her gently. "Do you need anything else? I can ask Pearl or another of the aunts for it if you do."

"I have a supply. I'll just take some aspirin."

"You know where it is." Augie had taken several that morning to deal with his hangover.

After he left, Dallas waited a few minutes, then watched out the window until his neighbors had all made their way to the community center. She again filled her pockets with the phone, lock-picks, and knife. The search would be risky in the middle of the day, but she had to do it. She wanted to find some evidence and get the heck out. Not only did she miss Cameron, whom she hadn't spoken to since she left, but she was starting to hate being here. Mostly because of the child abuse, she suspected. Another reason she felt compelled to check the shed again.

Outside, she hurried down the lane, holding her belly in case someone saw her. She walked right up to Jove's gate and let herself in, without glancing around. If anyone was watching, she wanted it to seem as though she had permission and nothing to hide. Dallas strode across the backyard the same way, heading straight for the sliding glass door. She cast a quick glance at the shed, but couldn't tell it if was still locked. Even if it was, she'd already released two pins, so it should be easy to access. If she had time.

No. She would make time by conducting only a superficial search for the journal. She hadn't been able get the metal box out of her mind, visualizing all kinds of creepy stuff. She wanted to open it, to see for herself that it was filled with nothing but tools then stop obsessing about it. That still left the *penalty box* unaccounted for, but she would press Augie about it tonight. The reference might be nothing more than a corner where he'd taken timeouts as a kid.

Out of habit, she glanced up for security cameras, but didn't see any. The glass door slid open easily and quietly. *Yes!* Inside, Dallas paused, listening for any sound or movement.

She crossed the kitchen quickly, turned into the hall, then made a beeline for the back bedroom. A king-sized bed took up half the space, the smell of sweat and sex lingering. Dallas jogged over to a tall dresser and rifled through the drawers.

Nothing noteworthy, except a collection of sex toys and a drug stash that included cannabis and amyl nitrates. Jove was quite the playboy. She checked the nightstand, expecting more toys, and found a Ruger handgun instead.

Her pulse escalated. The weapon made her nervous about being caught in the house. What if Jove carried one on his person too? Dallas checked under the mattress, then rushed to the closet and felt around the upper shelf with her hands. In the back corner, she came into a contact with a soft-bound book. She pulled it down, and her pulse jumped another notch.

A journal covered in sky-blue fabric with the initials KS handwritten in black marker on the bottom corner. The girl had started her diary while she was still Kenna.

Now what? Taking it back to the cottage to read was a risk. Not only would she have to hide it from Augie, Jove might discover it missing and freak out. Also, if it proved to be evidence in Zena's murder, Jackson needed to acquire it legally.

Dallas opened the journal and flipped to the back pages. The last few days of Zena's life mattered most, and Dallas knew she needed to get out of the house soon. Skimming the last page of entries gave her another jolt. Zena had written: *Going out to meet my father tonight. So excited!*

A scraping noise on the window made her jump, but it was only a tree branch blowing in the wind. Dallas pulled out her phone and snapped an image of the page, then took photos of the previous two, plus one of the cover. Reluctantly, she shoved the journal back into the corner and hurried out of the room. Maybe Zena's final notes would be enough to give the taskforce what they needed for a search warrant.

At the back door, she stopped, feeling a sudden urge to send the images now before she spent any more time on the shed's lock. If Jove or Craig caught her, they would seize her phone, and the vital information would be lost. Dallas accessed the burner's limited photo file and sent the images to Jackson, not bothering with a text message.

Outside, she gulped some fresh air and felt her pulse settle down. The worst risk was over. She already had an excuse ready if she were caught breaking into the shed: *She thought she heard a dog whimper and worried that it was trapped.*

Instinctively, she glanced around before pulling her lockpicks, then shook her head. Why would anyone be in Jove's backyard? Yet her nerves were pinging. She rarely had to do this kind of thing in broad daylight.

With her hands warmer than they'd been the night before, she was able to manipulate the last two pins into place within a few minutes. Dallas pulled the shackle out of the lock-body, then slipped the whole mechanism out of the latch. Carefully, she slid the shed's metal door open.

The stench hit her first, reeking like an outhouse. With no natural light, it took a moment for the scene to come into view. The front half of the dark space contained yard tools, but in the back, a portable metal crapper sat in one corner, and a small boy huddled in the other. No food, no water, nothing under him but dirt.

Dallas sucked in a painful breath.

The boy opened his eyes with a look of fear.

"Don't worry," she whispered. "I'm here to help you."

The boy stared, still unsure.

"Can you get up?" He didn't look restrained, but she suspected he'd been there since sometime last evening. His poor little legs were probably cramped or numb.

He whimpered as he stood. "Who are you?"

"Amber, a friend of Augie's. He sent me to get you."

The boy nodded, and Dallas held out her hand. She turned to lead him out, and her heart missed a beat. Jove stood in the opening. "I knew you were trouble."

Instinctively, Dallas shoved the boy past him and out of the shed. "Go!"

Before she could raise her arms to defend herself, Jove pulled a stun gun and fired two prongs into her chest. A massive dose of electricity surged through her body, a pain unlike anything she'd ever experienced. Dallas' legs buckled, and she collapsed to the ground. A second later, another shocking pain hit her, and her mind went blank.

Chapter 41

Monday noon

Jackson pounded up to the second floor of the courthouse and knocked on Judge Cranston's door.

"It's open," a gravelly voice called from within.

Jackson stepped inside. "Thanks for making time for me." He'd called ahead to make sure the old man was still in the building.

"I have a tee time in less than an hour, so make this quick."

Jackson launched right in. "A young woman is dead of a fentanyl overdose, but she's not a user. The injection went into her upper arm, not her inner elbow, so it seems as though someone else injected it." Jackson stayed on his feet, his sense of urgency growing. "She also recently left a dangerous, controlling cult, so I think she was murdered. The members live in a walled-off, gated compound. But I want to bring the leader, Jove Goddard, in for questioning." Jackson set the paperwork on Cranston's desk. "I need you to sign this."

The judge leaned back in his office chair. "Will you please sit while I skim it?"

Jackson obliged him. "We have an undercover FBI agent inside the compound, and she's funneling us information."

"Then what's the rush?"

"She thinks they're mutilating children. She saw one kid with no earlobe, and the dead girl was missing the tip of her finger."

"Good grief." Cranston looked over his glasses, his wrinkled face hard to read. "That's crazy. Do you have pictures?"

"No. But the overdose victim also had various old breaks and scars the pathologist said were typical of abuse, and his autopsy report is attached to the subpoena." Jackson handed him a second set of papers. "I printed out the agent's texts too. The cult members are anti-technology, so cell phones aren't allowed, and our agent has to be careful."

"Any other reports or confirmation of the abuse?"

"An ex-cult member came forward this morning and confirmed that Goddard is physically abusive. I've included a summary of her testimony." Jackson had tried to call Maddie back to sign a written statement, but she'd run and never looked back. "I limited the search request to Jove Goddard's house, but we'll gather more evidence, and I'll be back for a broad search of the whole place."

"Let me skim read." The judge pushed his glasses into place.

Jackson sat quietly, even though he wanted to pace. A few minutes later, he heard a notification on his phone and checked his texts. Another one from Dallas. No message this time, just an image of a handwritten page. Another photo landed. The cover of a blue notebook. Zena's journal!

"Excuse me, sir."

Cranston looked up.

"I just got photos from our agent. The dead girl's journal, which was taken from her apartment after she died, is in Jove Goddard's possession."

"Sounds like you need to bring him in." The judge signed the papers and handed them back. "Good luck."

As Jackson hurried down the corridor, he enlarged the first image and struggled to read the sloppy handwriting. Je thought it said, *Going out to meet my father. So excited!* The entry was dated the day of Zena's death.

He stopped in the hall and sent a group text to his taskforce: *Meet at the compound now.*

On the drive out, Jackson called Lammers and updated her.

"For fuck's sake. Maybe the girl *was* murdered." The sergeant paused and made paper shuffling noises. "Do you need more people?"

"That depends. If Goddard won't open the gate, we'll need the armored vehicle."

"I'll call Bruckner and get the SWAT unit on standby."

Fifteen minutes later, Jackson parked in front of the gate at the end of Louis Lane. None of his teammates had arrived, so he called them to ensure they were on their way.

Evans pulled up behind him as they were talking. "I'm here."

Schak and Quince were on their way as well. They'd been on standby since the meeting, waiting for the order. Jackson climbed out, his stomach rumbling. He'd missed lunch but didn't care. Adrenaline pulsed in his system, and he felt a little nauseous. With Evans at his side, he stepped up to the security box and rang the buzzer.

Like the time before, no one responded. He rang again and again with no response. "Keep pressing," he told Evans. "And stay off to the side." Jackson got back in his vehicle, noting Schak's arrival.

Jackson wished were driving a patrol SUV with a crash-guard bumper, designed for what he had in mind. Maybe if he did enough damage to this old sedan, the department would issue him a new unit. He pressed the accelerator and rolled forward into the gate, just hard enough to shake it. Evans stared at him open-mouthed, then grinned. Jackson backed up and rammed the gate again.

From the side, Evans gestured that they had a response.

Jackson jumped out and rushed over to the security post. Through the intercom, Goddard shouted, "What are you doing? You can't damage private property!"

"We have a signed subpoena and search warrant, and the armored SWAT vehicle is on the way to help enforce it. You can open the gate, or we will bust through."

"Hold the paperwork up to the camera. I want to see it."

Jackson didn't feel like indulging Goddard, but he wanted to keep this legal. He held up the part with Cranston's signature. "Open the gate!"

After a loud clicking noise, the metal barriers began to move.

Goddard shouted again, "I'll meet you out front! Do not bother the other members."

Jackson couldn't hold back a scoff. In time, the team would interview everyone in the cult. For now, they were focused on Jove and Augie Goddard. Jackson drove through and followed the asphalt until it stopped, then he parked in front of a large central building. As he got out, he scanned what he could see of the property—subdivisions with tiny houses, gardens, greenhouses, and a wooded hillside in back.

His teammates parked and climbed out too, watching as a tall, sandy-haired man strode out of the main building. "I'm Jove Goddard," he announced with arrogance, apparently not intimidated by the presence of four police detectives standing in his hidden world. Or maybe he'd learned to fake courage as part of his scam.

Jackson opened the back door of his scratched sedan. "Get in. You're coming into the department for questioning."

Goddard scowled. "Why can't we do it here? I have nothing to hide."

"Great, because we plan to search your home." Jackson waved the warrant. "Get in!"

The man hesitated. Schak and Quince stepped forward.

"Fine." Goddard moved toward the open sedan.

"Where is Augie?" Jackson asked.

Fear sparked in Goddard's eyes. "Why?"

His son was his weakness. Apparently even sociopaths could love their children. "We're taking him in for questioning too."

"That's unnecessary. Leave Augie out of this."

"Tell us where he is or we'll go door to door."

Goddard clenched his teeth. "Second house on the right." He pointed to a lane that ran beside, then behind, the community center. "You're wrong about me," Goddard whined. "I'll prove it when I sue you for harassment and win."

Jackson had heard that a few times. "Where's your house?"

Goddard let out an exasperated noise. "What are you looking for?"

"Zena Summers' journal."

The cult leader's eyes shifted, as if calculating the risks. "My home is behind this main building, and the journal is in my bedroom closet, in the back of the top shelf. There's no need to tear my house apart looking for it."

"Great. Get in."

Goddard finally complied. Jackson shut the door, then instructed his team. "Schak, stay with Goddard. Evans, go get the journal. Quince, take a quick look around for anything unusual. I'll round up Augie."

As they split up, Jackson wondered about Dallas, but he couldn't ask about her and blow her cover. Hopefully, she was still gathering evidence and testimony they could use to justify more search warrants and build a case against Goddard. Today's court order was specific to Goddard's house with a focus on the journal. Jackson would wait to hear from Dallas again and try to be patient about searching the whole compound. When he had the green light for that, he would bring the forensics team too.

Right now he had to find Augie Goddard.

Chapter 42

Back at the department, they put Jove and Augie into separate interrogation rooms, then stood in the lower foyer and planned their strategy. "Evans and I will question Jove, while you two interrogate Augie," Jackson suggested. "Then we'll confer and compare their statements. What do you think?"

"I respectfully disagree," Evans countered. "I think we should question Jove first and pressure him with pinning the murder on his son. Then do the same with Augie. He's already a wreck, and he'll probably break down. If he doesn't, we'll go back and use whatever he tells us to trap or crack Jove." She paused, still thinking. "Quince should take the journal to the conference room and skim through it, so he can feed us information as he finds it."

"I like it." Jackson nodded his approval, then glanced at Quince. "You didn't happen to see Dallas anywhere, did you?"

"No. But I saw the kid with the missing earlobe and tried to talk to his mother. She ran into her house and slammed the door."

"Based on what Maddie Drake told us, the mother likely made the cut herself, coerced by Jove." Jackson sucked in a breath, wanting to be in two places at the same time. "We'll get back to the rest of them soon. But first, we push the

Goddards to tell us what happened to Zena. And who the hell her father is."

Schak shuffled his feet. "Want me to babysit whoever isn't in the hot seat? Hang out in the room and make him nervous?"

Jackson smiled. "You were made for it."

He and Evans grabbed sodas from the breakroom, then hurried back downstairs. In the first interrogation room, Jove sat upright, staring straight ahead. *More false bravado?* They hadn't cuffed him or Augie, wanting their suspects to feel like they were just witnesses in an important case, not criminals. Jackson sat across from the cult leader, and Evans scooted past him to the inside chair.

Jackson zipped through the routine camera-recording notification to get it out of the way, then opened with diplomacy. "We appreciate your cooperation in this matter."

Jove scoffed.

"We're just trying to find out what happened to Zena Summers. Do you know her?" Testing the man's basic honesty.

"You know I do. She lived in our community up until recently." Jove cocked his head. "When I knew her, she was Kenna Slaney, daughter of Pearl Slaney."

They might have to bring in the mother too. "Do you know why she changed her name?"

"You tell me."

Smartass. Diplomacy time was over. "Where were you last Wednesday night, October first?"

"Probably at home." Jove held his finger to his mouth, another smug gesture. "Wait, no. I was at the university, attending a lecture."

Jackson didn't believe him, but the alibi would be nearly impossible to confirm or disprove. "What lecture and when was it over?"

"It was a series about global warming and sustainability and ran from eight until ten-thirty."

So he was downtown during the first part of Zena's time-of-death window. "What did you do when you left?"

"I stopped for a drink at Mac's, then went home. I probably got back to my house around eleven-thirty."

A crowded bar—also difficult to verify. "Did anyone see you arrive at home? Or did you interact with anyone?"

Jove's mouth curved in a self-satisfied grin. "Interact? You can call it that, but Pearl and I are more honest and just refer to it as fucking."

Pearl would probably lie for him. New tactic. "Your son, Augie, has no alibi for the night of Zena's murder. He also seems quite distraught and ready to confess."

Jove was silent, his expression stony. Finally, he said, "Augie's emotional, but he's not that stupid. Besides, he didn't kill Zena. He loved her."

Evans cut in. "Men murder the women they love all the time. You'll have to do better than that."

Jove gave a half shrug. "I don't have to do anything."

Jackson's phone beeped, and he quickly checked his messages. Quince had texted: *Z journal says Jove forced Uncle Craig to cut off fingertip.*

Bam! There it was. "Tell us about the time you mutilated Zena."

Fear flashed in his eyes. "I've never mutilated anyone."

"You didn't read Zena's journal after you took it from her apartment?"

No response.

"She claims you forced Uncle Craig to do it. Under Oregon law, failure to protect a child from abuse carries almost the same penalty as the abuse."

More silence.

Time to push his buttons. "You took the journal to prevent us from reading it. Why keep it? That seems foolish."

"I didn't kill Zena. I didn't take the journal."

"But we found it in your house."

Jove's expression tightened, but he didn't respond.

"So Augie stashed it there." Jackson nodded, as if putting it together. "He killed Zena, stole her journal, and—"

Jove abruptly stood and slammed the table with both hands. "Stop saying that!

Jackson shot to his feet and started around the table. "Sit down!"

Evans moved more quickly, cuffing the big man as Jackson shoved him back into the chair. "Get up again, and we'll bolt you to the floor."

Jackson gave him a minute to cool off, then asked, "Why was the journal in your house?"

Jove pulled in a quick breath. "Augie brought it to me."

He'd thrown his son under the bus. "You're admitting he killed her and stole the journal?"

"No! He didn't kill her, but yes, he took the journal because I asked him to."

"Why?"

Jove's breathing was labored. "As you already know, I didn't want you to read it."

Was his denial of Augie's part in the murder about semantics? "Did Augie *push* Zena to commit suicide?"

"Of course not. He loved her."

"Who supplied the fentanyl?"

"I have nothing else to say." Jove leaned back and crossed his arms. "Until I get a lawyer."

Chapter 43

Out in the foyer, Jackson looked at Evans. "What do you think?

"Augie killed her." Evans bounced on her feet. "But I think Jove instructed him to. He wanted Zena dead to silence her and confiscate the journal."

"Ruby mentioned that Zena planned to write a memoir," Jackson added. "That kind of public exposure would have destroyed the cult and sent him to prison for child abuse."

Jackson pounded on the second door to let Schak know they were ready to swap.

"Here's a question," Evans mused. "Why was Zena unafraid to spill the cult's secrets? He supposedly forced everyone to do something criminal or vile that he could hold over them."

"Maybe she got out before he could. Also, Zena didn't join the cult willingly. Her mother forced it on her, so she probably didn't have any loyalty to Jove."

Schak stepped out of the other interrogation room. "This kid is already crying. Breaking him won't even be fun." Schak grinned. "But messing with Jove will." Their partner did a skip step to the next door.

Jackson pivoted to Evans. "Ready?"

She nodded and keyed in the security code.

Augie sat with his head in his hands, but he looked up as they entered. His handsome face was puffy and red-eyed, but he'd gained his composure. "Jove has nothing to do with this. Please let him go."

The kid was obviously a better person than his father. Children who grew up being abused either became abusers themselves or vowed to be opposite of their parents. Sometimes, both things happened.

"Let's start at the beginning and go slow," Jackson said, sitting down. He noticed Augie had a bottle of water. Good. They wouldn't have any distractions. "But first, what did you mean by the word *this*? Jove had nothing to do with what?"

Augie blinked. "Zena's death. Isn't that why I'm here?"

"Yes. Tell us about your relationship with her."

"We were best friends growing up in the Path community, mostly because we were the only kids our age." His voice was steady, as though he'd made peace with his confession. "But eventually, we were bored and horny teenagers, so we had sex." He smiled sadly. "Then we fell in love."

"Whose idea was it to leave the compound?"

"Kenna's. I mean Zena." He shrugged. "Sorry, old habit. She was more adventurous—and bitter about being there."

With good reason. Jackson had so much he wanted to ask, but this was just the first round of questioning, so he would hit the highlights. "How were you treated as a child?"

"Mostly quite well. We had a simple, happy life."

"What about the penalty box?" Evans asked.

Augie crossed his arms. "I don't want to talk about that."

They would circle back. "Why didn't you move out with Zena?"

"I planned to do it slowly, over time, so Jove could get used to me not being there."

"Was he angry when Zena left?"

"Oh yeah."

"Did he threaten her? Or try to bring her back?"

"I don't know." Augie sipped his water and wouldn't look at them.

They would circle back to that too. "But you never moved out with Zena, and she started dating someone else."

"That broke my heart." Tears rolled down his face.

"What caused the breakup?"

Augie pressed his lips together and tried to get control. "Zena wanted to find her father, so she did the DNA thing with that 23 company."

"And?"

"I sent my spit in too, hoping to find my mother. All I knew was that she abandoned me." Augie's face crumbled in pain. "Instead, we learned that we had the same dad. We were half-siblings! Zena couldn't handle it and broke up with me."

Holy shit! Jackson and Evans glanced at each other, eyes wide. Their baby might have been deformed or mentally handicapped. Would they have known about that potential? Jackson had so many questions.

But Evans went first. "You're saying Jove is Zena's father too?"

Augie shook his head and started to sob. "I don't want to talk about that either."

Jackson spoke gently. "Will you tell us about the night she died? And explain why you killed her? It will feel good to get that off your chest."

"I didn't kill her! Yes, I was there, but I didn't know she was going to die. I could never hurt Zena." He broke into sobs again.

Chapter 44

Dallas blinked rapidly. *What was happening? Where was she?* Darkness all around her, and a cold dirt floor underneath. The shed! Memories trickled in—picking the lock, finding the child in the corner, helping him up. Then Jove! He'd been standing in the doorway with a taser, then he'd zapped her. Twice. No wonder she hurt all over, but her torso especially, as if someone had stabbed her with a hot fireplace poker.

She rolled to her side to relieve the pain, then tried to get up—and realized her wrists were bound. *Fuck!*

Calming breaths, she coached herself. Breathing slowly, Dallas sat up and held her wrists to her face. Her eyes were adjusting to the darkness, and she recognized her bond as a super thick twist-tie. The thin metal interior was coated with a heavy layer of rubber, giving it substance, but it was still a twist-tie. With some patience, she could free her wrists.

Dallas shoved the free ends into her mouth and almost gagged from the stink of the crapper in the corner. She hoped like hell she didn't have to use it before she got out of the shed. *And she would get out.* Dallas started the laborious process of rotating her bound hands in the opposite direction of her mouth and head movements. After a few minutes, her jaws ached, so she took a short break and decided to stand. Her legs buckled, and she collapsed back to the ground. Fifty-thousand volts of electricity—twice—did that to muscles. They would recover eventually.

For a moment, she sat and listened. In the distance, she heard voices, but they were moving away. Would anyone here defy Jove to help her? Augie might, but she hated to risk pounding on the walls and summoning the wrong person, like Craig. Could she overpower him? Not with her hands bound. Other members might hear her pounding and ignore it . . . or tell Jove.

How long had she been here? A better question was: *What did Jove have in mind?* Was this just a punishment for her as a member who'd violated the rules, or did he plan to take her out into the woods tonight and shoot her? She would've bet money on the latter. On impulse, she leaned over to the door and tried to slide it. Locked, as she'd expected. She started the untwisting process again.

Dallas had to rest her jaws twice before she finally undid the last twist and the rubber strap fell to the ground. *Yes!* Dallas flexed her numb hands for a few seconds, then placed them on the ground and pushed up. Her legs wobbled, but held. She waited a moment, then took a tentative step. All good. She could walk. Her torso felt like it was on fire, and she was tempted to check herself for wounds. Tasers could leave third-degree burns, but it didn't matter now. She had to focus on getting out.

Her head pounded, and she felt dizzy. *Damn.* She had to be able to think. More deep breaths. Slamming into the door seemed pointless. Metal sheds were often flimsy, but not this one. The padlock on the door wouldn't budge without a sledgehammer. Dallas stepped over to the stack of tools in the corner. Maybe there was something sharp, like pruning shears. She rummaged through a pile of shovels, rakes, and trowels. Could she punch through the metal with the pointed end of the trowel? *No.*

Dallas remembered that she'd brought a switchblade with her, but her pockets were empty now. Jove had taken her phone and lock-picks too. She shook her head, trying to clear it. She dropped to her knees and felt around in the dark corner in case she'd missed something. Her fingers latched onto something small and metallic, and she pulled out the object—garden scissors, the kind used for cutting through the thick stems of flowers. These could work.

Maybe.

She had to try, but where to start? Dallas began an inch-by-inch search of metal walls, looking for any kind of hole—a missing screw or an accidental puncture. If she found one, she would shove the tip of the scissors into it and twist until she'd enlarged the opening. When it was big enough, she would start cutting. If she didn't find a hole, she would shove the scissors under the sliding door and bend up until she had a gap.

If neither of those plans worked, she would wait until Jove came back and stab him in the neck. What if he wasn't alone? If his plan was to take her out and kill her, he would probably need help from Craig. Jove would have the stun gun too. Overcoming all of that would be challenging.

Oh hell. She had to get out before it got dark. Even if she got lucky and found a weak spot in a wall, cutting open a hole big enough for her body to climb through could take hours. Heart pounding, Dallas pulled junk away from the walls, searching for a sliver of hope.

Chapter 45

Jackson felt the room close in on him and took off his jacket. He had to be patient and let Augie tell his story in whatever way brought everything forward. He'd suspected that two people might have worked together—such as Dagen and his mother or Jove and his son—but now Augie was suggesting someone else entirely. Although he could be lying.

Jackson took a long drink of Diet Dr. Pepper, then asked, "Who else was there?"

"Our father, the guy we found through the DNA thing."

"Tell me his name."

"It doesn't matter now." Augie looked like he might cry again. "I'll always be an orphan."

Evans suddenly cut in, sounding angry. "Like hell it doesn't matter. Just tell us."

Jackson felt the same, but this troubled kid needed a gentle touch.

Augie's silence confirmed that.

Jackson backed up. Might as well get the whole story. "How did you and Zena and your biological father end up at Skinner's Butte?"

"It was her idea."

* * *

Augie remembered the day in vivid detail. How could he not? He'd met his biological father, then watched him murder the love of his life! The events played out in his mind, as they had, over and over, for the last four days.

After his shift at the garden store, he'd driven over to Zena's, unable to keep himself from seeing her. She'd been his friend, then his lover, and now, she was his sister. He would always love her.

Zena opened the door and smiled. "Hey, get in here. I have news." She grabbed his arm.

Surprised, Augie let her pull him inside. She'd sent him away the day before, saying they needed time apart to let their feelings cool off and become more 'sibling-like.' He glanced around her place to make sure Dagen wasn't there. The apartment was still mostly a big empty space.

"What news?" he asked. "Haven't we had enough of that?"

"I contacted our father, and he wants to meet us."

"What? I didn't expect that."

"Me neither, but it's what I wanted." Zena patted her belly. "I hope he likes the idea of being a grandpa."

A sick feeling rolled through Augie's stomach. "I don't think you should have the baby." He plopped down on the couch. "I talked to—"

Zena cut him off. "We've discussed this. I'm not getting an abortion."

"Hear me out. I talked to a smart lady at work and asked her about such things."

Zena shook her head. "You weren't supposed to—"

"I just asked her *What if,,* you know, like a hypo—." Augie stopped, unable to remember the word. Their homeschooling had been limited.

"I know what you mean." Zena nodded. "Go ahead. Finish."

"Anyway, she said the baby could be deformed or not right in the head."

"But maybe not. We're only half siblings." Zena paced the room. "I want this baby. If I can't have you, at least I'll have part of you."

Augie sighed. "At least you're not feeling suicidal anymore. That scared me."

"Everything out here scared me at first. But I'm free, and I'm not gonna waste it. I'll make a good life for myself and this child. I have big plans."

He admired her determination. "Where are we meeting this guy?"

"Skinner's Butte. You know I love it up there."

"What time?"

"At ten. He has to work until then."

"That sounds kind of weird." Augie was still upset that Jove wasn't his real father and had never told him. When Augie had confronted him, Jove had been pissed off and called him ungrateful.

"Not really," Zena argued. "I chose the place, and he went along with it. He also said he didn't want his wife to know just yet, so he didn't want to meet anywhere too public."

"Okay. I'll pick you up." Augie stood. "Does Dagen know about this?" Just saying the guy's name hurt.

"No. He doesn't want the baby either, so I'm easing out of that relationship."

Augie tried not to smile. "I have to go home and do chores. I'll see you tonight."

Later that evening, as they drove up the curvy road, Zena got nervous. "What if he tells us to get lost and stay out of his life?"

"Then that's what we'll do." Augie patted her leg on the seat beside him. "You knew the DNA thing was just a chance. We were lucky the guy was in their database and even luckier that he wants to meet us. Don't get your hopes up. This has to be difficult for him."

"I suppose." Zena was quiet for a minute, then said, "I wonder if he knew about us back then, you know? When he got our mothers pregnant."

Augie hadn't thought about that. "Maybe not. If he walked away then, why is he willing to meet us now?"

"Because we're adults and all the hard work is done."

Augie laughed. "Maybe you're an adult . . . "

The parking lot was mostly empty, except for a jeep-like vehicle along the front and possibly another car backed into the corner by the unity building. At ten o'clock on a weeknight in early October, that wasn't surprising. Augie parked next to the jeep. "Do you suppose that's him?"

"Probably." Zena reached for her door handle.

Augie glanced over, but he didn't see anybody in the SUV. "I don't think so."

He climbed out too, and they stood on the sidewalk, looking out over the city.

"I love this view," Zena said. "It reminds me that there's a lot I want to see and do, and that no matter how hard it gets, I'm not going back to the Path community."

Augie decided he should get out too. There were worse things than letting technology ruin his brain.

A voice called to them from below. "Hey, is that you, Zena?" The man stood about ten feet down the slope on a flat area.

"Sure is." She started down the narrow path.

Augie grabbed her hand. "Be careful." Their only light came from the moon and the city below. As they approached the man, his face came into view. Augie stopped and stared. He looked so familiar. Uncle D! What was he . . . *Oh shit.*

Augie finally found his voice. "Hey, I remember you."

"I wondered if you would." D laughed softly. "And now you know. I'm your dad, not your uncle."

"But why—"

Zena cut in. "You're Jove's real brother?" She turned to Augie. "Did you know?"

"Of course not. Another of Jove's secrets." Augie felt lightheaded and confused, but sort of happy too. At least his biological father wasn't a total stranger who would reject him.

"I'll never be free of him," Zena cried out, anguished.

Augie knew that she meant Jove. He squeezed her hand. "Jove doesn't have to know."

"Except for the baby."

"You're pregnant?" Uncle D sounded surprised and upset. "Is that why you're here? You want money?"

"No." Zena was upset too.

Augie wanted to leave. To get drunk and forget all this. He had wanted to find his mother, not his father, and D had never even been a good uncle, disappearing out of his life when he was a kid. Augie would never think of him as *Dad.* "Let's go." Augie tugged Zena's hand.

"Not yet." She stepped toward D, taking out her phone as she did. "Why did you leave my mother and me in the compound? My childhood was hell!"

Their father didn't respond.

Zena stepped closer and confronted him face to face. "When I write my book, you'll look just as bad as all the other adults in Simple Path. Maybe worse." She lifted her phone and took his photo.

Uncle D suddenly slapped her. Zena's hand flew to her face in shock. D grabbed her phone and pocketed it.

Before Augie could step in and pull her back, D swung his other arm up and slammed a fist into Zena's shoulder.

"Oww! What the hell?" She burst into tears.

Augie reached out to Zena, but D pushed him, and Augie tripped, nearly losing his footing.

Uncle D pivoted back to Zena and shoved her hard. She stumbled backward toward the slope. D lunged and pushed her again. Zena tripped and fell, then rolled, crying out as she hit the ground.

Augie regained his balance, but couldn't think straight. "What are you doing?" He started down the hill to help Zena.

But Uncle D pulled him back. "I just did you a huge favor for you." He held out his open palm and revealed a syringe. "She'll die very quickly, and it will look like an overdose. No one will ever know we were here."

"Die? You killed her?" Panic surged in Augie's chest, and his heart raced. "Why?"

"She would have ruined both of us." Uncle D squeezed his arm. "You're my son, Augie. I've always known that. I'm sorry about letting you go, but your mom and I had split up, and she wanted to stay in the Path community." He paused. "And

Jove wanted a kid." D made a bitter noise in his throat. "And what Jove wants, Jove gets."

Yeah. But none of that mattered now. Zena was gone! "What did you give her?"

"A powerful opioid." Uncle D started up the hill, pulling him along.

Augie was too stunned to resist.

"I came prepared," D said, "because I expected her to make trouble, just like her mother. But I didn't want to use it." He shook his head. "She was gonna write a book about the cult, about her life. If I had let that happen, the world would have known you screwed your sister and had a baby with her. I want you to have a better life than that."

"But you killed her!" Augie burst into tears. "I have to get out of here." He pulled free.

Uncle D slapped him hard. "Don't be stupid. If you say another word about this, now or later, I'll pin her murder on you. I have the power to do that."

Oh shit. Augie's mind spun. Zena had been murdered with an overdose, and his crazy uncle was threatening to set him up for it. Heart pounding, Augie turned and ran up the slope. D was a cop and could get away with anything.

Chapter 46

Jackson sat back, stunned by Augie's story. What cop? What if the whole thing was fiction? A made-up boogie man to get Augie and Jove off the hook. "What's your uncle's name?" *A man who was biologically his father.*

"It doesn't matter now."

Why did people keep saying that?

"Tell us," Evans demanded. "Zena needs justice."

Jackson pulled out his phone to text Quince. Maybe Zena had identified their biological father in her journal. But Quince had already texted him: *Zena's dad is Darren Mitchell!*

The murdered police officer? What the hell? Jackson showed the text to Evans. "Let's regroup."

Upstairs in the conference room, they strode to the monitors that displayed the interrogation rooms. Quince glanced at them, then looked back at the screens. On one, Augie had his head down again. On the other, Jove sat upright, defiant.

Quince shook his head. "Officer Mitchell as a killer? I never knew him, but still, one of our own? I'm having a hard time with this."

Evans snapped her fingers. "Maddie Drake. She abandoned her child at the compound and never mentioned her ex-husband's name. I'll bet she's Augie's biological mother."

"Call her and confirm it, then get her back in here."

Schak hustled into the room. "What did I miss?"

Evans gave him the update. "Officer Darren Mitchell is Zena's father and killed her to silence her." She paused. "If Augie is telling the truth about what he witnessed."

"What?" Schak's mouth dropped open. "I don't believe it." He slumped into a chair. "Darren was my friend. How sure are you about this?"

Quince touched his shoulder. "Zena named Mitchell in her journal, and Augie says he witnessed the murder."

Schak shuddered. "I guess I didn't really know him, but now that I think about it, Augie looks just like him."

Jackson couldn't focus on that now. "We have to confirm Augie's story." He turned to Evans. "Talk to Mitchell's wife again. See if she'll verify that Mitchell went out Wednesday night."

"We need to hit the compound again first," Evans countered, "and question Pearl about Zena's father. We have to question all the members about everything."

"Yes. I meant later for Sloan." Jackson turned to Quince. "Book Augie into jail for obstruction of justice, for starters."

"What about Jove?"

"Him too. He admitted he told Augie to go get the journal, so I'm sure he knew his brother murdered Zena." Feeling overwhelmed, Jackson took a breath. "Hell, Jove may have even plotted the scheme with Darren. He had just as much to lose if Zena wrote and published her memoir."

"We may never know," Schak said.

Jackson nodded at him. "I need you to update my subpoena with a request to search the whole Simple Path community. Take it to Cranston, wherever he is. Evans and I will head out there now. If someone lets us in, we can get started." Jackson needed to update Sergeant Lammers too, but he shared Evans' sense of urgency about getting back into the compound. He wanted to find the penalty box and get technicians out there to document the evidence.

Quince started to leave, but Jackson grabbed his arm. "Ask Augie about the penalty box and text me if you learn anything."

"Have you heard from Dallas?" Evans asked.

Jackson glanced at his phone. "Not since I got the photos of the journal." Since all her texts had been arriving late, he had no idea when she'd actually sent them. "I'm sure Dallas is fine, but we'll look around while we're out there."

Schak rubbed his head. "I wouldn't count on someone letting you in. We may need the SWAT truck to bust open the gate."

"You're right." Jackson gestured at Schak impatiently. "Go get that warrant signed and text me the minute you have it."

"Will do." His partner hustled out.

Evans bounced on her feet. "I'll head over to Second and Chambers while you get Lammers and Bruckner on board."

"Good plan. See you out there." Jackson gave her arm a light squeeze. "Maybe we'll get to celebrate with a drink later this evening."

"Not if you don't get moving."

As he rang the buzzer at the compound, Jackson knew he was wasting his time. Still, it was better for the department's reputation if they didn't have to barge in, especially since they didn't have a pressing need to enter. No one armed—that they knew of—and no one's life was at stake.

Unless a child was in the penalty box right now or at risk of mutilation, they could take a moment.

No response at the gate. After ten minutes and three tries, Jackson stepped back. They would do it the hard way. A moment later, Evans texted him: *On way with Barney. Clear the access.*

Jackson jumped into his sedan, backed it down the lane to a gravel turnout, then texted Schak: *Don't park in front of gate. SWAT truck on way. Any update?*

As he walked back to try the buzzer again, Schak responded: *Got it. Green light to enter.*

Chapter 47

The rumble of the armored vehicle was a distinctive sound—a loud engine combined with massive tires rolling up the road. Jackson tensed, suddenly worried. He jogged over to the gate and shouted, "We're coming through! If you're near the gate, get back! I repeat, get away from the gate!"

He prayed no one in a vehicle suddenly decided to leave. He hoped Bruckner, or whoever was driving, had the good sense to go easy and brake on impact. Knowing Evans, she was likely in the passenger seat and had described the compound's layout. That would help minimize collateral damage.

Jackson spun away from the gate and ran to safety. A moment later, the big blue truck rolled into sight, accelerating rapidly, with Bruckner driving and Evans riding shotgun. The armored vehicle slammed into the gate with a thunderous impact. The gate flew off its track and landed flat, then Barney rolled right over it.

Bruckner braked and skidded to a stop where the pavement ended inside the compound. Jackson rushed through the opening on foot.

Evans was already climbing out. "What's the plan?"

"We find and search Augie's home. We find Pearl and pressure her to help us. Put her on ice in the back of my sedan if she won't."

"Should I start in the community center, then fan out from Jove's house and go door to door?"

"Exactly. Schak and Quince will be here soon." Jackson pivoted and yelled at Bruckner, who was still in the truck. "Thanks! Be on standby." For what, he didn't know, but this compound might hold some disturbing secrets.

Evans was already running for the center, and Jackson jogged after her.

Inside the main building, they found two women in the kitchen. "Eugene Police," Jackson shouted. "Where is Pearl's home?"

"What's going on?" The older member crossed her arms. "You were here earlier and took Jove. Why?"

"Pearl's daughter was murdered. Do not interfere with our investigation, or we'll charge you too. Where is she?"

The woman's lips trembled. "The house nearest the garden." She pointed west.

"What about Augie? Does he have his own place?"

"The beige cottage behind Jove's."

Jackson started toward the door, then turned back. "What about Amber, the new member? Where is she?"

The older woman shrugged, but the younger one stepped forward. "She's been staying with Augie, but I haven't seen her since this morning."

Jackson nodded and kept moving. They conducted a quick search of the building, but found only a small group of children upstairs in a school room. He would get social workers out here to question them soon.

As they hustled back outside, Jackson said, "I'll check Jove's place again, and you go find Pearl's house. Bring her to the center for questioning."

"I'm on it." Evans ran toward the houses on the west side of the property.

Jackson jogged around the community center to Jove's house behind it. The front door was unlocked, so he hurried inside and conducted a quick check of each room for witnesses and weapons. Nobody was in the house, but in the master bedroom nightstand, he found a handgun. *Damn!* Quince had missed it earlier when they'd been focused solely on the journal. But Zena hadn't been shot, so the weapon was likely irrelevant. Jackson pocketed it anyway, not wanting a member to potentially use it against anyone on the team.

He searched the dresser drawers for more weapons, but instead found a stash of drugs and personal sex items. Jackson left it all for the technicians to bag and tag as evidence.

When he'd cleared the house, Jackson decided to look at the backyard. He opened the sliding door and stepped out. A metal shed along the back fence caught his attention. *The penalty box?* He jogged across the lawn and stopped in front of the padlocked door.

What was that sound? Like metal on metal, coming from inside the shed. He tapped the door. "Who's in there?"

"Jackson?" The voice came from a back corner.

Dallas! "Yes. Hang on, I'll be right back." Jackson sprinted toward the armored truck. This rescue needed entry tools, maybe even the doorknocker.

Chapter 48

Later that evening

Exhausted, Evans drove toward home. The celebration Jackson had mentioned would have to wait. They'd spent hours at the compound, identifying everyone, asking top-tier questions, and arranging for later, more-lengthy interviews. Then she'd had to get a ride back to the SWAT station and pick up her own vehicle. Now she just wanted to be done for the day.

Yet something nagged at her brain. Darren Mitchell had reportedly murdered Zena late Wednesday night, then had been shot and killed by a criminal the next morning. That was rather instant karma. The sequence of events was certainly possible. Police officers worried about their lives every day. Evans shook it off, remembering that a second officer, also investigating the human trafficking gang, had been shot and survived. In addition, those thugs had fired on Schak and Quince. The case was closed. Still, she would feel better about the whole wrap-up after she talked to Mitchell's wife.

Impulsively, Evans pulled into a parking lot and turned around. Why not do it now before the taskforce meeting in the morning?

As she rolled up to the Mitchells' house, Evans sensed movement inside. *Good news.* Sloan was home, and she could get this over with. Evans parked on the street, hurried to the entrance, and knocked. The widow took her time responding, then only opened the door a few inches. "It's late. Why are you here?"

"I have some news about your husband, and it's important." Evans tensed, thinking about how devastated the woman would be to learn her husband had been a killer.

For a long moment, Sloan just stared with watery eyes, then finally opened the door. "I'm not sure I can handle any more."

"I understand, and I won't take up too much of your time."

"Detective Evans, correct?"

"Yes."

Sloan Mitchell led her into the living room and gestured at a guest chair. "Have a seat." The widow sat on the end of a plush couch and propped her feet on an ottoman. A bottle of wine sat next to her on the end table. More like half a bottle. *Good, she'd been drinking*, Evans thought as she sat down. Maybe it would make the news easier to bear.

"Just tell me. What's so important?" Sloan seemed to brace herself.

Evans decided not to sugarcoat it. "A young man told us he witnessed your husband, Darren Mitchell, commit murder Wednesday night."

"What?" The widow looked surprised but not shocked. "Murder who? You mean an armed criminal?"

"A girl named Zena Summers. We've confirmed through DNA that she was Darren's daughter."

"That's crazy." Sloan shook her head, then gulped some wine.

"He also had a son from his previous marriage." Evans wished she had a beer. This was about to get ugly. "Do you know Darren's ex-wife?"

"Not personally. I didn't know he had adult children either." Sloan's face tightened. "He told me he didn't want kids."

"Did you know Darren had sent his DNA to 23andMe for analysis?"

"We both did. He wanted to prove he had some Native American blood." Sloan shook her head. "That's how you know about his children." She leaned forward to get up. "I've had enough bad news for one night."

Evans wasn't done. "I'm sorry to put you through this, but I have a few more questions. We need to confirm a few details about Darren's movements."

"Like what?"

"Did he leave the house Wednesday night?" *Or had he been working a patrol shift?*

"He did." Sloan rubbed her temples. "I remember, because the next night when you told me he was dead, I wondered where he'd gone." For a second, bitterness ruined her beauty. "Darren went out a lot. I thought he was cheating on me."

Maddie, his ex, had called Darren an adulterer too. As well as an abuser. Evans made a mental note to get back to that. "What time did Darren leave?"

"I'm not sure, but I think around nine or so. He said he planned to get a drink at Lucky's."

"When did he come back?"

"I don't know. I went to bed." She gulped more wine.

That didn't ring true, especially if Sloan thought her husband was out with another woman. "Had Darren cheated on you before?"

Her expression shifted to anguish again. "Probably, but he was clever."

So she had tried to catch him cheating in the past, which meant Sloan likely hadn't gone to bed after her husband left. Jumbled thoughts slammed together in Evans' brain. What if Sloan had followed Darren that night, thinking he was cheating on her? Then saw him kill Zena?

"Clever how?" Evans asked, trying to buy herself time.

"Never mind." The widow finished her glass of wine.

Evans' thoughts kept rolling, pulling together the backstory and motive. Darren had been a mean, shitty husband. Sloan might have even learned about his now-adult children and resented him even more. He'd apparently denied her the kids she wanted. Sloan already had several reasons to hate him, but then she'd witnessed him murder a young girl, his own daughter. The poor woman had probably snapped. Killing the bastard might have seemed easier—and more advantageous—than reporting his crime. The investigation, the public humiliation, and the loss of his benefits. Why not forego all that and have her husband die on the job as a hero?

"Are we done?" Sloan stood, glaring at Evans.

"Please sit down."

The woman let out an exasperated sigh, sat back in her chair, and poured more wine.

"Where did you learn to shoot?" Evans asked.

Sloan tensed, then scowled. "What are you talking about?"

Evans decided to abandon the line of questioning. They would never be able to prove Sloan had done anything. She was crafty, even shooting at another officer to make sure suspicion fell on someone else. But Evans wanted to know anyway. "Let me lay out a scenario of what I think really happened."

"I'm not interest—"

Evans cut her off. "When Darren left the house, you followed him to the butte and saw him meet with Augie and Zena. You may have even overheard the conversation. But seeing him murder that girl sent you over the edge. He had cheated on you, physically or verbally abused you, and lied about his past. Then he committed murder and made you a witness."

Sloan shook her head, but didn't speak.

"Rather than report him or confront him about the crime, you decided to take justice into your own hands. You apparently knew Darren's schedule for the next morning and simply had to lay in wait." Evans shook her head and forced herself to sound casual. "Why put yourself through the stress of a trial? Having to sit there in court and be a supportive wife. By killing him, you got rid of a husband you hated, saved yourself public humiliation, and earned his survivor's benefits."

A sly smile played on Sloan's face. "If any of that were true, and it's not, you couldn't prove it."

"I'm not sure I want to." Evans nodded, her feelings jumbled. "I've been abused, and I know how you felt." *Mostly true.* Her own father had beaten her badly enough that she'd thought about killing him once or twice. Evans cocked her head. "But shooting at a second officer? That was bold and risky."

Sloan shrugged and drank more wine.

The woman's failure to deny it, or even act offended by the accusation, confirmed Evans' suspicion. But it would be impossible to prove. Sloan had likely used an untraceable rifle, tossed it in the river, then spent the whole day covering her tracks. Or maybe she'd met with a client afterward to establish an alibi. The burner phone Darren had used to contact Zena was probably in a creek or landfill.

Evans shook her head, knowing this woman would get away with murder. Lammers considered Mitchell's homicide closed and wouldn't want to hear any of this. A judge would never authorize a subpoena for either of the Mitchells' phone records or financial information. Evans' theory, though solid, was dead in the water.

Sloan leaned toward her. "Did I mention that the district attorney is my good friend?" Her speech was slurred now. "He won't appreciate hearing this nonsense, and he certainly won't ever press charges. You might as well let it go. Pursuing this fabrication will only make you look bad."

Evans stood, knowing Sloan was right. This theory and conversation would go with her to the grave. Evans wanted to tell Jackson, but it wouldn't be fair to him. The knowledge and powerlessness to act on it would drive him crazy. She loved him enough to spare him that.

Chapter 49

Tuesday, Oct. 6, 8:45 a.m.

At his desk, Jackson checked his email. He'd called 23andMe again when he'd first arrived at work, and the CEO had promised to send Zena's DNA profile and correspondence immediately. Jackson had been busy since, updating his case notes. Summarizing Augie's testimony had taken most of the morning, and he still had Dallas' report to read and include in the file. But the team was meeting in a few minutes, so he was out of time.

The message from the biologics company landed as he stared at his overflowing inbox. Jackson opened it, downloaded the PDF, and started printing. He didn't have time to read it first. He printed his case notes too, gathered up all the documents, and headed for the conference room.

The team was already inside, talking quietly. Jackson took a seat at the head of the table and passed out the case notes. "These don't include Agent Dallas' report, but she'll be joining us." He held up the DNA papers. "We also have Zena's file from 23andMe, but I haven't read it."

Evans reached for the file. "I'll skim it now."

As he handed it over, Dallas walked in. "Good morning, my fine fellow officers of the law."

"You're in a good mood," Jackson commented, "for someone who was locked in a shed all afternoon."

"But I'm not now, and Jove Goddard is in jail, so I'm good." Dallas sat down. "I would've eventually cut my way out, you know."

"I have no doubt. We've added kidnapping to Jove's charges." Jackson smiled. Dallas and Evans were both amazing. He was lucky to work with them. "Will you start us off by summarizing your observations and conversations?"

Dallas nodded. "I texted the important details as I learned them, so the only other major occurrence was finding the little boy locked in the shed. I was specifically looking for the penalty box Augie had mentioned." She let out a small laugh. "I didn't expect to end up locked in there myself." Dallas rubbed her chest, likely unaware of the motion. "The fucker tased me twice, and I may end up with a scar on my boob."

Jackson had tried to take her to the ER, but she'd refused and had shown them around the property instead. Which reminded him . . . "I have some bad news." Everyone looked over, startled. "Joe Berloni called me this morning from the compound. A technician found bones near where the wall is being built. He's pretty sure they're human. And young."

"Damn!" Dallas shook her head. "I had a bad feeling about that place the moment I arrived."

"Thanks for taking the assignment," Jackson said. "You gave us the breakthroughs we needed. And very quickly."

"It's what I do." She scowled. "Or maybe not. I'm thinking of quitting the deep undercover work. If you stay in it too long, it changes you."

The room was quiet for a moment.

Jackson glanced at his notes. "We have many more interviews to conduct and asking about the bones and the mutilations will be a priority." They'd arrested Craig Ronson, the man Zena had accused of cutting off her fingertip, but the DA's office would likely not prosecute him. Nonsexual child abuse had to be reported within twelve years, or so he thought.

Evans suddenly looked up. "This report confirms that 23andMe sent Zena a text referencing two close relatives, Augie Goddard and Darren Mitchell."

"I wonder if Mitchell got a similar email about Zena and Augie," Jackson mused.

Evans nodded and looked away.

"Ruby claimed that everyone at the compound was promiscuous," Jackson added. "So I wouldn't be surprised if there are more interrelated members." He looked around. "What else have we got?"

"I stopped by the jail this morning like you asked," Schak said. "I got Dagen released and asked him about the fentanyl patches. He admitted to taking them from his mother's stash and giving one to Zena to hold for him."

"Thanks." Jackson suppressed another wave of guilt for how he'd treated Lisha Hammersmith, but he'd just been doing his job. He glanced at Evans. "Did you, by any chance, talk to Sloan Mitchell last night?" Knowing Evans' energy and drive, she probably had.

"Yep. She confirmed that her husband left the house between nine and nine-thirty."

"That fits." Jackson nodded. "Did she say anything else? Did she know about his adult children?"

"If Sloan did, she wouldn't admit to it." Evans' voice was deadpan. "I think Darren Mitchell kept a lot of secrets."

"Apparently, that ran in the family," Schak joked.

Lammers stepped into the room. "Sorry I missed the meeting, but I'll read your reports." She walked over to Jackson and held out her hand for a copy. "Anything critical I need to know before my meeting with the chief?"

"We'll need cadaver dogs to search the compound property," Jackson said. "We found a set of bones."

"For fuck's sake." The sergeant clapped him on the shoulder. "You were right to bust into the place. Well done."

"Thanks. It was a team effort."

Lammers gave a thumbs up, then grimaced. "Officer Mitchell's funeral service is tomorrow afternoon. Most of the department doesn't know the truth about him yet. I can't decide if I should announce it now or wait."

"You should tell everyone," Evans said. "Give them the option to not attend. I'm not going."

"You're right. I will."

It would be crushing news for the patrol officers who'd worked with him, but Jackson concurred. They had the right to know. He looked around at his team. "After interviews today, let's go celebrate wrapping up these cases."

Chapter 50

That evening

Jackson strode into the Sixth Street Grill, a favorite hangout from before the department moved, and spotted Dallas at a table. Surprised that she'd showed up, he hurried over. "Glad you could make it." Jackson sat across from her.

"My flight was cancelled." She smiled ruefully. "Otherwise, I'd be on my way back to Flagstaff."

"I wouldn't blame you. Your gigs in Eugene tend to be dangerous." In addition to being shot during her last trip, she'd once infiltrated a local eco-terrorist group and had almost been blown up.

"All my gigs are dangerous." She gave him a slow smile. "I suspect you're an adrenaline freak too."

"Maybe." Jackson ordered a beer from their server, thinking he might drink the whole thing this time. It had been a rough five days.

Evans showed up and sat next to him. "What are we drinking?"

"Pliny the Elder." Dallas held up her glass. "Voted America's best beer for seven years running."

"I'll have one." Evans signaled the server and ordered three. "Schak and Quince will be here shortly."

Jackson glanced at her. "I thought Schak quit drinking."

Evans laughed. "His bouts of sobriety are like his diets and plans to retire—good intentions only."

The guys showed up just as their beers did, and Schak took a long drink. "Man, that's good." He nodded at Jackson. "Thanks."

Jackson pointed to Evans. "She ordered it."

"But I'm buying," Dallas said. "This celebration is on the bureau. You took down a dangerous cult, and my boss appreciates that."

"You think they'll disband?" Jackson was skeptical.

"Without their leader? Always." Dallas sipped her beer. "I also looked into their financials and mortgage information this afternoon. Simple Path was going broke. The main organization, SEL, had cut them off."

"I'm sure Jove was already working on his next scam." Jackson shook his head. "But between the child-endangerment and kidnapping charges, he'll be in prison for ten years or more."

"He'll only be fifty-something when he gets out," Evans commented. "Then he'll probably start right back up again."

Dallas let out a half snort, half laugh. "I finally realized why he calls himself Jove. It's the name of a Roman god, and Augie is short for Argus, one of Jove's mythological sons."

"Oh hell," Schak mumbled.

"So yeah," Dallas continued. "James Grabski is a megalomaniac narcissist who will get out of prison, change his name again, and start a new following. He can't help it."

A depressing thought. Time to move on. Jackson raised his drink in a toast. "To our good work!"

They clinked glasses and downed a swallow. Then Evans recounted her ride up to the compound in the armored truck and gave a moment-by-moment description of breaking through the gate. "It was electrifying!" She grinned. "Bruckner loved it too and let out a yell as we smashed into it."

"Damn!" Schak pouted. "And I was stuck with getting papers signed."

Jackson chuckled. "Your wife bribed me to keep you on the sidelines."

Schak shot him a look. "I don't care. I'm thinking of retiring."

They all laughed.

"Right after you quit drinking," Evans said.

"And lose twenty pounds," Quince added.

Jackson grinned, pleased to see his team relaxed and happy. They didn't get many moments like this.

An hour later, everyone had left but Evans. Jackson smiled at her. "I'll walk you out."

On the way to her car, she asked, "How is your family?"

This was his opportunity. "We're in transition. Kera and I split up."

Evans stopped walking and turned to look at him. "What happened?"

"Her ex sued her for custody of Micah, and she decided to work things out with him."

Evans looked disappointed. "So Kera broke up with you." She started walking again.

Jackson grabbed her arm. "Wait. No. I had already decided not to move into the rental with Kera."

"No? Why not?"

"I realized I wasn't in love with her."

Evans sucked in a sharp breath.

Jackson pulled her in and kissed her deeply, whispering, "I realized I'm in love with you."

"It's about time."

L.J. Sellers writes the bestselling Detective Jackson mysteries—a four-time Readers Favorite Award winner. She also pens the high-octane Agent Dallas series, the Extractor series, and provocative standalone thrillers. Her 28 novels have been highly praised by reviewers and readers alike.

Detective Jackson Mysteries:

- The Sex Club
- Secrets to Die For
- Thrilled to Death
- Passions of the Dead
- Dying for Justice
- Liars, Cheaters & Thieves
- Rules of Crime
- Crimes of Memory
- Deadly Bonds
- Wrongful Death
- Death Deserved
- A Bitter Dying
- A Liar's Death
- A Crime of Hate
- The Black Pill
- Silence of the Dead

Agent Dallas Thrillers:
- The Trigger
- The Target
- The Trap

Extractor Series:
- Guilt Game
- Broken Boys
- The Other

Standalone Thrillers:
>No Consent
>The Gender Experiment
>Point of Control
>The Baby Thief
>The Gauntlet Assassin
>The Lethal Effect

L.J. resides in Eugene, Oregon where many of her 28 novels are set and is an award-winning journalist who earned the Grand Neal. When not plotting murders, she enjoys standup comedy, cycling, and zip-lining. She's also been known to jump out of airplanes.

Thanks for reading my novel. If you enjoyed it, please leave a review or rating online. Find out more about my work at ljsellers.com, where you can sign up to hear about new releases. —L.J.

Made in the USA
Monee, IL
23 May 2022